FREE TO LOVE

BOOK ONE:
THE CHANDLER'S DAUGHTER
ALI SPOONER

BOOK TWO:
FORBIDDEN LOVE
ANNETTE MORI

Free To Love

Book One:
The Chandler's Daughter
Ali Spooner

Book Two:
Forbidden Love
Annette Mori

Affinity
Rainbow Publications

2018

Free to Love
© 2018 by Ali Spooner & Annette Mori

Affinity E-Book Press NZ LTD
Canterbury, New Zealand

1st Edition

ISBN: 978-1-98-854927-9

Editor: CK King aka Raven's Eye
Proof Editor: Alexis Smith
Cover Design: Irish Dragon Design
Production Design: Affinity Publication Services

ACKNOWLEDGMENTS

ALI SPOONER

I would like to thank my fans for following my stories, providing great feedback and encouragement. Writing wouldn't be so much fun without you. Thanks to Affinity Rainbow Publishing, Irish Dragon for the cover art and the team of editors, readers, and publishers who continue to help me grow as a writer. Thank you to Annette Mori for joining me on this fun story.

ANNETTE MORI

First, let me thank Ali Spooner who allowed me the great honor of working with her on this project. A huge thank you to all of my beta readers: Gail Dodge, Danna Micoletti, Ali Spooner, Carrie Camp, Ameliah Faith, Dana Holmes, Elle Hyden, Linda North, L. Ann Hill, and Lyss Wolf, who made great suggestions to improve the initial draft. As always, I have to acknowledge Erin O'Reilly who is a constant support and encouragement to me. I am honored to call her a friend and have her support me in my journey. I would also like to express my gratitude to Affinity Rainbow Publications and the wonderful trio (JM Dragon, Erin O'Reilly and Nancy Kaufman) who continue to provide feedback to tighten up manuscripts that need assistance and publish my unconventional work. I am eternally grateful for the opportunities they give me to let my stories see the light of day. My other family members who are also very supportive, include my nephew, Aaron and his wife, Chelsea, my two sisters, Kim and Val, and my father who struggles to read my books with one eye. I always enjoy working with the beta editor Nancy Kaufman who helped tighten our stories. Thanks to CK King for her magic as the final editor to tighten the story even further. She is a delight to work with. Inevitably, there are those pesky final errors that slip through and I am thankful that the final proof editor, Alexis Smith, caught those before the book went to print. Thanks to Nancy Kaufman for the final cover. Nancy is also a promoter extraordinaire. A huge thanks to all the other readers and fellow writers who have sent personal e-mails, written reviews and posted nice things on Facebook (you know who you are). The Affinity authors are an especially supportive group and often share posts or send words of encouragement. Finally, my wife, Jody, continues her support even when it interferes with our time.

DEDICATION

ALI SPOONER

To Bubba, the best brother a girl could ask for. Thank you for sharing so many adventures with me. I hope we will have many more together.

ANNETTE MORI

To all the strong women in history who continue to fight for our rights to live an authentic life. To my wife who I love dearly for her patience and ability to take care of me when I fail to do that myself.

TABLE OF CONTENTS

ALSO BY ALI SPOONER

Single Stories

Christmas Story (Affinity's Christmas Medley)
Diamond Dreams
The Bee Charmer
Ruined
Back in the Saddle
Open Your Heart
South of Heaven
Shotgun Rider
The Settlement
Love's Playlist
Cowgirl Up
Twisted Lives
The Epitaph
Terminal Event
Bailey's Run

Series

The Island Series
Neptune's Ring
Venus Rising

The Hunter Series
Bound
The Devil's Tree

Sasha Thibodaux Series
Sugarland
Bayou Justice
Line of Sight

ALSO BY ANNETTE MORI

Unconventional Lovers

The Organization

Captivated

The Termination

The Review

The Ultimate Betrayal

Locked Inside

Out of This World

Asset Management

The Incredibly True Adventure of Two Elves in Love
(Affinity 2014 Christmas Collection)

Love Forever, Live Forever

The True Story of Valentine's Day

Vampire Pussy...Cat

Nicky's Christmas Miracle X3

(*It's in Her Kiss*, (Affinity's Charity Anthology)

Who is Nicolas Clause? (Affinity's Christmas Medley)

Book One

The Chandler's Daughter

Ali Spooner

CHAPTER ONE

Cecelia DuPont's eyes scanned the fog-enclosed surface of the Savannah River, searching for the rowboat that would bring her lover back into the harbor city. A chilled breeze filled the salty air of the brisk November morning. The sun had risen hours ago, but the low cloud cover shrouding the city caused the fog to linger. Awakened from her slumber, Cecelia hoped the dreams of her handsome lover were an omen that Captain Blythe's ship would return from the Outer Banks.

The path running beside the docks and the launches tied there was still lit, as she paced the river front. A young man began to extinguish the oil lamps that had lit the way for thirsty sailors bringing goods into the harbor the night before. She nodded as he passed, his smile making the gloomy morning a bit brighter. Her eyes scanned to the southeast, to the Tybee Island lighthouse guiding ships into the mouth of the Savannah. Yes, the spermaceti candles were lit to illuminate the tower. Lighting the tower in 1791 had allowed Savannah to become a bustling port city.

Cecelia's eyes caught movement on the water, and her heart plummeted when she saw the small ship the crew moored to the pilings. She stared at faces filled with misery, as bound and shackled Africans were herded onto the cobblestone path that would take them to the slave market. She shivered at the ugliness her city harbored, separating children from parents, and spouses from one another, to be sold into slavery to tend the white man's cotton fields in neighboring states. The despair in their deep, black eyes called to her as she watched them shuffle through the rough streets.

An overseer from the market cracked a whip at a young boy no more than ten years of age. "Pick up your feet, damn you, skinny little cur," he growled. The boy's eyes shined white with fear, as he regained his feet.

"He's just a little boy," Cecelia cried out to the filthy man.

"Mind your own business, missy." He growled at her and spit a stream of tobacco juice in her direction.

She was uncertain if the enslaved people could comprehend the language, but the looks given to her from several of the adults made her think they understood her intent.

"Get your eyes off a white woman," he screamed and lashed the closest man to him, rending shirt and skin.

"Careful with the merchandise, Morgan," a deep voice called out.

Cecelia turned when she recognized the voice. "Merchandise, Uncle Walter?"

"Yes, my dear girl. These people are merchandise, just as the cotton they will be picking, which will be baled and sent to market in Virginia."

"But they are human beings, Uncle, and should be treated fairly, not enslaved and sold to the highest bidder," came her retort.

"Without slaves, the southern plantations would not thrive, and our tiny, little family business would die. It's survival of the fittest. They work the fields, and are given food and lodging. Surely, you don't expect whites to harvest the crops?"

She watched the group shuffle into a barracoon. The cement, tunnel-like structure would house the slaves until they sold at market. *Like a herd of livestock.* She shuddered at the thought.

Cecelia felt bewildered by his response. She had always respected her uncle, who owned the chandlery with her father. She had no idea her family engaged in the practice of selling humans into slavery. The knowledge appalled and nauseated her.

"What are you doing down by the riverfront this morning anyway? Are you not working at the shop today?"

She looked up at him, a defiant fire in her eyes. "I'm just stretching my legs. I'm not due to arrive at the shop for a little while yet."

"Don't be long. We have a multitude of shipments coming in today that will require proper inventorying, and a load of cotton to be shipped to Virginia."

His comment made her heart smile. She knew that Captain Blythe would, more than likely, deliver their shipment of cotton. Cecilia walked along with him to the family store on the riverfront. Her father was already bent over a stack of papers when they entered. He looked up and smiled at his only child.

"Good morning, Cecelia. I'm glad you made it; we have an awful lot of work today."

"That's what Uncle Walter was telling me. Where should I begin?"

He handed her a stack of papers. "You can start by organizing these orders. Once they arrive, we'll need to start recording the inventory and arranging for the local deliveries. Captain Whaley has been waiting on this new rudder for weeks now. If it arrives today, please send word he can pick it up, or we'll arrange for delivery tomorrow."

"Yes, Father, I will." She took the stack of papers to her small desk to begin the sorting. Her attention perked, when her father asked his brother, "Is Captain Blythe still scheduled to take delivery of the cotton for Virginia?"

"Yes, she assured me they would arrive by midmorning and depart on the morrow."

Damn, just one night with her. One night would just have to be enough.

Cecelia had first met Captain Hillary Blythe two years earlier, when she began delivering their cotton to Norfolk. The dashing young captain, recently relocated from England, sailed the most modern ship available for commerce in the Americas. When she wasn't delivering cotton for Cecelia's father, she was delivering rum, spices, or other products from the Caribbean islands. Her tales of the crystal-blue waters and enchanted isles had seduced Cecelia from their very first encounter. Cecelia dreamed of leaving

Savannah one day, to set sail for one of the tropical islands Hillary talked about.

"A new shipment of Africans also arrived this morning," Walter told his brother. "A right sorry-looking lot, but I reckon they will have to do."

Cecelia flinched at the harshness of his words and looked at her father to gauge his reaction.

Cecil frowned at his brother's words. "I understand their plight is a necessary evil for the plantations to prosper, but I do wish the owners would provide better care and arrangements for them."

She was proud of her father for speaking his mind.

"They are marginally better than beasts of burden," Walter said. "From what I hear, the jungles and plains they are taken from provide no better means of survival. Here, at least, they are fed and sheltered."

"Yes, but at what cost? I hear the overseers can be brutal, and the plantation masters take such liberties with the women and girls." He glanced quickly toward his daughter, apparently remembering that she was in the room. "I'm sorry, darling, I forgot you were here. You should not be exposed to such conversation."

Walter slammed his fist on the table. "You are beginning to sound more and more like those northern sympathizers, Brother. Slaves provide necessary labor to produce the fabrics to allow those damned Yankees to parade around in all their fineries. Without them, southern plantations would revert back to mere sharecroppers, barely able to keep their families fed and clothed."

"I understand your plight, but have you truly no moral compass left or compassion for fellow human beings?

Certainly, our mother and reverends taught us better." Her father's face grew red with anger.

"Our reverends greedily scarf up every gold and silver piece that gets tossed in the offering plate on Sunday," Walter argued back. "They, too, benefit from the plight of slave labor."

"I cannot argue that."

Her father had so easily given up the argument with his older brother. Cecelia was relieved when the door opened and Anthony Page strode into the shop. Page was Hillary's first mate.

"I understand there is a load of cotton to be delivered to Virginia." He smiled at her father.

"There is indeed, sir." Cecil pushed a stack of papers aside and offered his hand to Page. "It has been a few weeks, I trust the crew has stayed out of trouble," he teased.

"We've just returned from the islands, taking a load of rum and spices up to Boston. The seas were a bit rough, but we were not shipwrecked. Captain Blythe knows these waters better than any man I've ever sailed with."

"She is a steady captain and a good businesswoman to boot," Cecil said. "Will she be coming ashore?"

"That she will. She has new wild tales to spin for Miss Cecelia," Page said with a wink to her.

"Tell her not to be filling my daughter's head with all those fanciful voyages. She's much too precious to go sailing off into the sunset on a grand adventure."

"Now Father, you know I wouldn't do that," Cecelia protested.

"Ha! I've seen the sparkle in your eyes after she's woven her whimsical tales."

She sighed. It was a good thing her father didn't understand that the captain herself made his daughter's eyes sparkle, not her wild tales. "You have to admit, Father, it tends to get a bit boring around here, staring at bales of cotton and equipment for ships and such."

"I won't argue on that. Maybe if you'd settle down with a good lad, that might add some excitement to your existence," he teased.

"I'm not prepared to become an old brood mare for anyone just yet."

"Careful. Your mother would die if she heard you talking such nonsense," he warned. "She's got several fine candidates already selected for you."

"Hmmmfffff," Cecelia groaned and resumed her paperwork.

"Has your crew dropped your ballast stones?" Walter asked.

Page smiled at him. "We've dropped a fair amount in anticipation of a good load of cotton. I'll be bringing the crew 'round to begin loading shortly, if you're prepared."

"That we are," Cecil answered. "We've got big shipments of supplies arriving soon, so we could use the extra space. When you return, Cecelia and I will come out to supervise the loading."

"I shall see you soon then." Page bowed slightly and left the shop.

†

Time slowly tormented Cecelia, and when the door opened for Hillary and Page's return, she felt time stand still. She could gaze into Hillary's blue eyes forever.

"Good to see you again, Captain Blythe," Cecil said, as he walked around his desk and shook her hand.

"Likewise, Mr. DuPont, I trust that you've been in fair health."

Her fine English accent was music to Cecelia's ears. Her focus drifted to Hillary's blond hair, just brushing her shoulders, as she animatedly spoke with the owners. Cecelia wondered if the handsome captain had grown even more beautiful in her absence. The deep tan of her exposed skin spoke of long days spent at sea and further accentuated her brilliant, blue eyes.

Hillary's gaze met Cecelia's. "I hope you will allow me to take you to dinner tonight, Miss Cecelia?"

"I'll look forward to that. We've a great deal of work ahead of us this afternoon, but I'd love to join you later."

"I guess we'd better get to loading some cotton then." Hillary's eyes sparkled. "Mr. Page, let's get our crew moving."

"Yes, Captain." He grinned.

"We'll see you in the warehouse." Hillary tipped her hat to Cecil and spun on her heel to follow Page from the office.

Walter watched her leave, then growled to his brother. "That woman irritates me with her cockiness."

"She's the best captain we've ever worked with. By far, the most reliable and fastest to deliver our loads," Cecil reminded him.

"I know. It's a sad state of affairs when the best is a woman, a foreigner at that," he grumbled and went back to work.

"You could always purchase a ship, Brother."

"That may be an option in the future, but not for now."

Cecil winked at Cecelia. "I prefer being a landlubber, but you're more than welcome to try out your sea legs, if you think you could command a ship."

Cecelia could barely restrain her laughter, as her father taunted his brother.

"Let's get this damned cotton on the ship." Walter growled and walked out of the office.

Cecil grinned at his daughter. "Somehow, I just can't see him on a ship. He turns green whenever we take a ferry across to South Carolina."

"Be nice, Father." She snickered, and followed him to the warehouse.

†

Cecelia watched, as Hillary supervised and assisted her men in moving wagons filled with large, cotton bales to the docks. She'd been impressed with the speed and efficiency of the crew as they cleared a large space in the warehouse. When the final wagon emptied, her crew left it at the dock to be loaded with the supplies anticipated later in the day. Hillary walked over to Cecelia.

"It is good to see you, my friend. I'll be taking the ship just out of the docks to anchor down for the night. When we are all settled, I'll return to take you to dinner."

"I'm looking forward to hearing some of your new tales." Cecelia smiled.

"Alas, the islands are so beautiful. I wish I could show them to you instead of telling you about them. Their beauty, like yours, is well beyond mere words," Hillary whispered to her and watched as the color flushed up Cecelia's neck and into her cheeks.

"You're such a smooth talker, Captain Blythe."

"But, it's the truth on both accounts." She smiled. "I'll see you soon."

Cecelia watched the handsome captain leave, then decided to make contact with Captain Whaley about the pending arrival of his rudder. "Father, if you don't mind, I'll go speak with Captain Whaley. I would like to stretch my legs a bit."

"Would you mind some company?"

"Why, of course not."

"We'll be back soon, Walter," he called out to his brother.

He held out his arm for Cecelia, and she looped her hand around his elbow. "Is everything all right, Father?"

"Yes, darling, why do you ask?"

"You don't usually accompany me on my errands."

"Can't an old man take a stroll with his only daughter?" He feigned a pout. "Besides, it has turned into such a pretty day."

"That it has. May I ask you something, Father?"

"Of course, you can."

"Are we now involved in the selling of slaves? Uncle Walter calls them merchandise. I wasn't aware we were doing that." She watched the frown cross his face.

"We are only providing temporary housing in one of our older warehouses. I pray that is the only involvement we have in that business. I don't agree with it at all, but Walter jumped all over the money offered for a barracoon."

"Those poor people. Half of them looked starved, and they all were terrified. I can't imagine the horrors that await them in our world."

Cecil sighed. "I agree, but there's nothing we can do about the practice. It's too ingrained in the South."

"That still doesn't make it right."

"No, darling, it doesn't, but if we don't provide them shelter, they will be out in the elements until they are sold on the block, or housed in much worse conditions. While I can't guarantee the warehouse is weatherproof, it has to be the best option."

When they reached Captain Whaley's office, he turned to her. "Do you want to enjoy the sunshine while I go take care of business?"

She smiled up to him. "Thanks, Father."

She sat on a small, rock wall outside the office and enjoyed the feel of the sun and soft breeze on her face. In the distance, she could see Hillary's ship slowly make its way from the docks, leaving room for a large, heavily loaded ship to enter the port. That would be the shipment they had been awaiting. The larger ship crept into the harbor.

The door to the office opened, and her father returned. "That looks like our delivery."

"I was thinking that too. She's riding low in the water, so it must be a heavy load."

"It will take most of the afternoon to get it stored and inventoried."

"I guess we should get ready then." She smiled at him and took his arm.

†

The afternoon heat and the activity in the warehouse made a trickle of sweat roll down Cecelia's spine, as she climbed carefully through the stacks of goods to confirm the inventory of delivered supplies. She was relieved when Captain Whaley arrived to take delivery of the rudder. She returned to the office to retrieve the invoice for him to sign, while the men loaded the rudder onto his wagon.

"All set," she said, when she took the invoice back from him.

"I can't wait to get back on the water." He smiled.

"Safe travels." She returned the invoice to the office, before resuming her inventory. Her father and uncle were busy inspecting two loads, when the final wagon was drawn into the warehouse. Cecelia walked to the stacks of supplies she had been working on before the rudder delivery. The diminishing space and the hustle had increased the heat in the warehouse. A fine patina of perspiration covered her skin, as she looked up at the large stack of burlap rolls used to bale the cotton.

†

Hillary ensured the safety of her ship and cargo, before returning to the waterfront with the majority of her crew. Two men remained onboard to protect the cargo, but she promised to relieve them so they could join their mates for some relaxation and more than a few pints of the local ale. She planned to bring Cecelia onboard after dinner, enabling them to spend some time alone in relative privacy.

"I can return to the ship if you'd rather stay in town," Page told her, as they walked to an Irish pub.

"Thanks, but Cecelia and I will return, so I can tell her of all our adventures." She smiled at her first mate. Her smile was short-lived, as moans of pain grabbed her attention. Her eyes followed the sound to the barracoon they were approaching. The falling darkness dulled her vision into the dark tunnel, but she could see movement inside, the momentary flash of white eyes as they looked away from her gaze.

The smell of human waste reached them, exacerbated by the heat of the crowded building. She turned to see Page looking too, before he turned back to her. "No human should be treated like that."

"I agree, but there is nothing we can do for these unfortunate souls."

"If only there was another way to harvest the crops, then this degradation of humanity wouldn't be necessary," he growled.

Calls from her crew walking ahead of them pulled her attention from the barracoon. The disgust she felt didn't dissipate as she walked away. Instead, it boiled deep in her soul. *There has to be something that can be done.*

Page held the door for her, and she walked inside to lay down the coins to buy her crew's first two rounds of ale. They cheered heartily, as the mugs passed around. Hillary took one in her hand and followed Page, away from the noisy men, to a quiet table.

She took a deep drink from the frosty beverage and placed the mug on the table. The plight of the slaves weighed heavily on her mind. She looked at Page. He knew her well enough to know she was scheming.

"What's on your mind Captain?"

"Have you ever given thought to becoming a pirate?"

"A pirate? Whatever do you mean Captain?"

"Page, I'm sure you know exactly what a pirate is. I'm talking about taking something from someone that does not belong to them. Very dangerous to even think it, but I admit the thought is running rampant in my head right now."

He leaned in closer, so only she could hear. "You're talking about the slaves, aren't you?"

She nodded. "I can't stand to think about the plight that awaits them. No man has a right to enslave another for their profit." To her surprise, Page didn't reel away in horror.

"You're serious about this aren't you? You realize, we could end up on the wrong end of a lynching, hanging from that big oak tree if we're caught."

"I know, I'm just thinking."

"If you are investing time to think it through, I know this is something you're passionate about. I'm a young and single man, with little to lose. Count me in on your plans. I can't speak for the rest of the crew. Especially those with families."

"That does play huge in any consideration. We can't do this with just the two of us." She grinned. She finished her drink. "I'm going to check on Cecelia. I'll see you later tonight. Enjoy yourselves, but remember we have a delivery to make."

"We will, Captain. You too. We won't be late."

Hillary left the pub and walked to the chandler's office. The warehouse was dark as she passed by, but lamps were burning in the office. As she approached, the door swung open and Cecelia and her father stepped outside.

"Good evening, Captain. You have great timing; we've just finished for the day."

"I hope you're still interested in dinner and conversation, Miss Cecelia."

"I'm famished. Father worked me hard today." Cecelia smiled at her father.

"Indeed, I have. Enjoy your meal, ladies. I'm heading home." He tipped his hat to them and started up the steps leading from the riverfront.

"Let us go find something to feed that appetite of yours," Hillary said, as they began walking the riverfront path.

Cecelia looped her hand around Hillary's arm as they walked. Hillary led them to a path as far away from the barracoon as possible, but the sound of moans still drifted across the air.

Cecelia recognized the source of the sound. Tears glistened in her eyes when she looked up at Hillary. "My heart breaks for those unfortunate people."

"Mine too." Hillary nodded and kept them walking. "The islanders are much like those imprisoned here, and they are such a delightful people. No man should be treated in this manner."

"I agree, but I know of nothing that can be done. They are such an integral part of the survival of the plantations."

"I understand your feelings about their plight. Maybe something good will change for them soon." Hillary sighed. "We can only hope."

"I hope you are right."

†

Hillary led them to a small boarding house that also hosted a simple tavern. Wonderful aromas met them at the door, and Hillary breathed deeply. "I smell good food. I bet they have fresh shrimp cooking."

"That we do, good captain. Come inside and we'll get you a seat. Hello, Cecelia. Aren't you worried about your reputation, being seen with this scallywag?" The woman teasing them chuckled and waddled toward an empty table.

"I think my reputation is intact, Ruth. Just don't tell Mother I'm going to have a pint of your ale."

"My lips are sealed. Make it two?"

"Yes, please, Ruth."

Ruth returned with two mugs and placed them on the table. "We have a special treat tonight, if you're interested. One of the fishermen who boards here caught a small tuna in his nets. They make beautiful steaks for grilling."

"I haven't had fresh tuna in a long time," Hillary answered.

"I'm not sure I've ever had it."

"We must remedy that then. We'll have two please, Ruth."

†

After dinner, they returned to the riverfront and rowed out to the ship. The two crewmen assigned to protect the shipment were relieved of duty to join the rest of the crew at the pub. Hillary tossed them each a silver coin to buy their first rounds.

When the men had left, Hillary lifted Cecelia onto a bale of the soft cotton and climbed up beside her. "Such a beautiful night to share with you," she said, as she settled next to her.

Cecelia sighed. "Not a cloud in the sky, and the moon is bright over the water. Even a nice breeze for us to share." She looked into Hillary's blue eyes. "Thank you for a wonderful dinner."

"It was my pleasure. I love my crew, but they aren't near as beautiful to share a meal with as you."

"Such a smooth talker, my dear captain."

Hillary's lopsided grin filled her face. "There is so much I'd love to share with you about my world. The many wondrous places I've traveled. I'm sorely tempted to kidnap you and take you to live at the islands."

"I'm not sure it would be kidnapping. I'd willingly go anywhere with you."

"I'm sure your father would not approve of that decision."

Hillary felt Cecelia's soft touch stroke her face. "Do I need to remind you that I am of age to make decisions that impact my future?" She laughed softly.

"No, my dear, you don't." Hillary leaned down, and her lips brushed Cecelia's with a soft kiss. "However, I don't relish hanging from the town tree, when he claims I've kidnapped you."

"Father would never do that."

"I'm thinking about doing something that, very easily, could lead me down that path."

She saw the confusion that crossed Cecelia's face. "What are you thinking?"

"Those poor slaves. They did nothing to deserve their plight."

"I agree, but what does that have to do with you?"

"A seed of thought has been planted in my brain, and I can't help but nurture it when I see them or hear their moans of agony. I know I have passed more than one slave ship in my travels."

"I still don't understand."

"Under the right circumstances, it wouldn't be that difficult to overtake a slave ship and confiscate their human cargo. I have a fast ship and could deliver the captives to the islands, to safety, to begin new lives in freedom."

Hillary watched, as Cecelia realized what she was saying. "You would become a pirate and risk your life for them?"

She nodded. "Someone has to do something to change their plight."

"But it would surely lead to a hangman's noose if you were caught."

"I do have to take that into consideration. I'm not completely convinced, but I am leaning in that direction."

"It's an admirable thought, but it comes with great risk. I'd die if anything bad happened to you."

"I have made enough fortune to live comfortably in the islands, and have already bought a parcel of land with a small villa."

"Why not retire then?"

"I'm not sure I would be happy, knowing I refused to help even a small number of them to live freely again. My conscience would eat away at me, knowing I could have helped at least a few."

She felt Cecelia shiver. "Are you cold?"

"No, I'm sorry. A chill ran down my spine at the thought of the peril you are considering."

Hillary moved to sit behind her and pulled her close, wrapping her in strong arms. "There's no need to fear. I think this is part of my destiny."

†

Cecelia turned her head, looking up and pleading for a kiss with her eyes. Hillary lowered her face to Cecelia's and kissed her deeply, eliciting moans from Cecelia. A caress down her arm and a brush along the curve of her breast, just beneath her dress, and Cecelia gasped at the feel of Hillary's palm cupping an ample breast with a gentle squeeze. "I wish there was time and privacy for more of your sweet intentions," Cecelia spoke in a near breathless voice.

Cecelia felt Hillary's hand move down the front of her dress as her tongue plunged deeply inside her mouth, making Cecelia's head spin deliriously with desire. She felt Hillary tease the dress upward to reveal the many layers of undergarments, she teased aside to explore the bare skin and soft mound of her womanhood. The panic of such exposure receded, as Hillary's fingers located the wetness that revealed Cecelia's desire. Gentle fingers entered her opening, sliding deeply between her walls. She felt her muscles clench against the invasion of her core, adding more wetness, encouraging deeper penetration. She kissed Hillary passionately and guided her hand to knead her swollen breast.

Hillary's groan felt as deep in Cecelia's mouth as the fingers moving deep inside her body, and her tongue danced wildly in response. She felt her inner muscles grasping for Hillary's touch as fingers slid in and out of her, moving faster and deeper. Her hips arched up with each stroke, and as the convulsions began, pleasure overtook her restraint. Hillary's kiss swallowed the loud moan that ripped through Cecelia as her release exploded. Hillary stilled her hand and kissed Cecelia more tenderly, as she began to calm.

"That felt so good," Cecelia whispered.

"Yes, it did." Hillary smiled, her blue eyes sparkling. "Can you stand?"

Cecelia nodded. "Yes, I think so."

"Good." Hillary jumped down from the stack and walked Cecelia to the back side of the stack of bales, facing the open water. "Sit here, and lean back."

Cecelia leaned back on her cotton-bale seat, her legs dangling over the edge, and stared up at the sky full of stars. She gasped when Hillary lifted her dress, lowered, and removed the undergarments allowing her to duck her head beneath the skirt to move between Cecelia's spread legs. She felt Hillary's fingers parting her lower lips and thought she would die when Hillary's tongue lapped at her juices. "Oh, dear God," she cried out.

"Quiet now, my dear," Hillary spoke in a brief pause, then returned to her feast. She buried her face in Cecelia's wetness, her tongue exploring deeply, as her hands reached up to knead Cecelia's breasts. She drank greedily, seeming lost in her own passion, until Cecelia clamped her thighs tightly around Hillary's head and erupted with pleasure, then collapsed onto the bale.

Smiling through the juices that coated her face, Hillary looked upon Cecelia. Her breasts were heaving, as she gasped for breath, and her eyes were glazed with pleasure. Hillary took her hands and pulled her to a seated position, pulling Cecelia into her arms for a deep kiss.

Cecelia was beyond bliss when Hillary kissed her. She could taste her own pleasure on Hillary's tongue, as she kissed her hungrily. The sensation was beyond description. When she broke the kiss, Hillary was still smiling. "You're quite pleased with yourself, aren't you, my captain?"

"I cannot deny that I am, sweet miss."

Cecelia slid down from the bale, slid her undergarments back on and took Hillary in her arms, spinning her and pressing her backward into the stack of bales. "Now it's my turn," she growled, as her fingers freed the belt from Hillary's trousers, and her hand plunged inside. Her fingers sought the heated wetness between Hillary's thighs and slipped easily into her center. Her mouth found Hillary's, as she began thrusting her fingers deep into her, eager for Hillary to feel the intense pleasure she had just given Cecelia. Hillary's hips began to rock into her hand, as the kiss grew hungry with passion.

†

Hillary was enjoying Cecelia's aggressive nature as she drove her backward into the bales and her hand hit the desired mark. Her hips instinctively rocked into her lover's hand, as their tongues danced passionately. She felt her climax rising rapidly, with each thrust of her hips. The taste of Cecelia's passion in their mouths was delicious, feeding her desire. She felt her body coiling for an explosion that triggered when Cecelia's thumb started brushing across her swollen pleasure pearl. Hillary could no longer hold back and released her climax into Cecelia's waiting hand.

Once their breathing returned to normal, Hillary fastened her trousers and retrieved a bucket of water to rinse their faces and hands. She had just dumped the bucket overboard when she heard the first of her crew returning. "That was good timing." She grinned. "I guess it's time to walk you home."

"I hope my legs hold out." Cecelia grinned back at her.

She led Cecelia to the boarding plank. "Welcome back boys," she called out, as the first group stepped on board, still merry from their reveling.

"Good evening Captain," Page called out to her. "I hope that you've had an enjoyable evening."

"Indeed, we did Page, but now that you're back on board, I think it's time I walk Cecelia home."

Page smiled, noting the flush on Cecelia's cheeks. "Do you want me to row you back ashore and wait for you?"

"Thanks Page, but I can manage this. Stay and make sure the crew returns safely."

"I'll see you when you return, Captain."

†

They left the ship and after securing the rowboat, started walking through town. Hillary intentionally took a route that would bypass the barracoon, unwilling to spoil the pleasant evening they had shared. She enjoyed the feel of Cecelia's hand on her arm, as they casually strolled through the squares in the heart of Savannah. The moonlight made shifting patterns across the cobblestones, as it bled through the leaves of the large oak trees. "Thank you for a truly marvelous evening."

"I would say it was all my pleasure, but I know differently." Cecelia chuckled at her mischievous quip.

"Indeed, it was as much my pleasure as yours. I hope it won't be long before we shall have the pleasure again."

"When do you think you shall return to our fair city?"

"It may be several weeks, depending on the weather. After we drop your father's shipment in Virginia, we'll be heading back to the islands for a cargo to return to Boston. Maybe by then, your father will have another shipment of cotton ready."

Cecelia held tighter to Hillary's arm. "I certainly hope so."

As they entered a rather dark section along their path, Hillary stepped away from the street and took Cecelia in her arms for a final deep and passionate kiss. Her home was merely another block away and this would be their last opportunity for a lover's embrace. "I will count the days until my return for more of your sweet kisses."

"I will be eagerly awaiting you. Please, come back to me safely."

"I will do my best, dear lady. Now, I must escort you home. We will be gone by first light, but your kisses will linger on my lips to urge me to return as quickly as I can."

When they reached Cecelia's home, Hillary turned to her. "Thank you again for a lovely evening."

"Likewise, I look forward to hearing about more of your adventures."

"Good night, Cecelia."

Hillary turned to walk away, then stopped to ensure Cecelia had made it safely inside. A fresh breeze had picked up, bathing her face. She strode confidently back through town to the riverfront, a decidedly energized bounce in her step. *What a beautiful evening.*

She stepped back onto her ship and found Page. "We need to set sail at first light. Do we need to go rescue the rest of the crew?"

"The last two returned just moments before you did, Captain. All of the crew is safe and secure in their bunks."

"I think we should follow them and get some rest. We have harrowing reefs to navigate in the morning."

"I'll be right in, Captain. Good night."

"Good night, Page."

Hillary retired to her private quarters and stripped down before slipping a nightshirt over her head. With the faint taste of Cecelia on her lips, she would fall asleep wearing a smile on her face and dream of her beautiful lover.

CHAPTER TWO

The next morning, the men were a little less cheerful as they lumbered onto the deck. With red and swollen eyes, they began preparations to lift sails and head for Virginia. The first few hours of their journey would be the most treacherous, as they navigated the coastal reefs to reach open water. It would take at least four days of sunrise to sunset traveling to reach Norfolk, if the winds remained constant. The jagged coast and hidden reefs were deadly to run during full nightfall, so Hillary decided to lower the sails and anchor after darkness set in. She had seen the evidence of numerous shipwrecks along the route. She would not jeopardize crew, ship, or cargo to make the journey any faster. She was not due for a week, so she was not pressed for time.

The morning blossomed into a beautiful day, as she watched the coastline carefully and listened for a cry from the lookout of any obstacle ahead. Several fishing boats headed out to sea, in search of their daily catch, and she smiled at the graceful, but loud, flock of seagulls that followed. The skies grew dark by afternoon, and Hillary barked out orders to cover the cargo. The crew raced into action and finished just as the first drops began pelting the deck. Her beautiful day was quickly turning into a miserable evening. She nodded to Page, and he began directing the crew to lower the sails. They had gone as far as they would for that day, Hillary preferring to set anchor and ride out the storm. She hoped it would pass during the evening and they would be underway again in the morning.

With the ship secured, Hillary joined Page and the others below. They sat around the table, enjoying a meal of stew and soda bread, as the storm raged outside. She surveyed the faces of her six-man crew. For several years, each of them had been willing to take on whatever shipments she desired, but never before had she asked anything of them that was illegal, risking life or imprisonment.

Her two married sailors were both from Norfolk, and she would not ask them to endanger their families by becoming pirates. That would drop her crew to four, plus herself. She would need to determine the size of the slave-ship crews, to weigh the odds of a diminished crew overtaking another ship. Hillary had seen a ship leaving Savannah with a crew of three men and a captain. If that was typical, she felt it would heighten their odds. The element of surprise would work in her favor, striking under the cover of darkness. She would launch the other crew in the ship's rowboat, while the captives were loaded onto her ship. Then her crew would lift the sails, take the slave ship farther down the coast by a mile, and anchor it there. If her plan worked perfectly, no man would come to harm. The other crew could row to their ship after she and her crew were safely underway.

If the timing was right, she could run down a slave ship. Her best opportunity would be southbound, after leaving Norfolk with a load of tobacco for Cuba. *What to do with the captives?* The ships she had seen held up to fifty prisoners. Her deck could easily accommodate a group of that size, but concealing them below deck for an extended period would be a problem. Her mind reeled with possibilities.

The men broke out a deck of cards for entertainment. She declined their offer, choosing to spend the evening scouring maps of the coastline. She knew most of the geography well, but she had never entertained a clandestine mission that would call for the unloading of humans under cover of night. *Am I insane to even be considering this?*

†

Strong winds helped them make up lost time the next day. When the sun began to set, she located a small harbor to anchor in for the evening. The leftover stew was heated and served. Hillary silently wished for one of the tuna steaks she had shared with Cecelia. When they reached Norfolk, she'd make sure the men got a solid meal in their bellies before they headed south. Just two more days to a decent meal.

Once the card game began, Page and Hillary returned to the deck to check the cargo and the ship's security. Page likely knew her recent silence meant she was in deep thought. His suspicions were accurate.

As they sat on a bale of cotton, she turned to him. "I've been thinking more about becoming pirates. Our two crewmen that are married with families are both from Norfolk, so we could leave them there while we make a run for Cuba with the tobacco. We'll go on to the islands for a shipment bound for Boston. If we were to run across a slave ship, we could board her in the dead of night and catch the crew by surprise." She looked up to find him listening intently. "From what little I've seen, the ships have a small crew of three to four men that we should be able to overtake with a surprise attack. I guess, with their captives bound and shackled, there's no need to have a larger crew, costing the captain more money and driving up the price of delivery."

"What plans do you have to protect our identity?"

"Facial wraps to conceal ourselves. Unfortunately, my accent would not only give away my gender, but my nationality as well. You would have to give the commands. For those missions, you would be captain."

"Good practice for my future endeavors." Page smiled.

"Which leads me to my next thought. I've purchased a small banana and cane plantation in the islands, and I've saved enough to live comfortably there. Would you be willing to purchase the ship from me and make payments during your routine visits?"

She watched his head snap up to look at her. "I would indeed, Captain. It would be my dream come true. I know the steadiness and speed of this ship but could never dream of affording to purchase or build one like her." He turned farther toward her. "When would you expect to be doing this?"

"Soon. I'd say within the next few months."

"If you're planning your retirement, why risk becoming a pirate?"

"A very good question, Page. I think to settle my conscience by doing something to fight against slavery. One, but no more than two raids would free a good number of slaves and would minimize any long-term risk to the crew and ship."

"I don't think I would carry on with the piracy after you retire."

"Nor would I expect you to. This is my lunacy, but I feel it is something I must do."

"Have you given thought to arming the men with pistols? I know you have one, as do I. To make your plan work, we would need several more."

"I have given that thought. I plan to walk into town to purchase guns and some supplies, while you supervise the unloading of the cotton and securing the tobacco cargo for Cuba."

"When do you want to approach the men with your plan?"

"I thought tomorrow night, after our meal. If they do not wish to partake, they can remain in Norfolk until we return."

"What if the married men insist on staying?"

"That, I will not permit. I will not endanger the welfare of their families."

Page nodded and remained silent for several long moments. "What of Miss Cecelia? Will she be accompanying you to the islands?"

"I can only hope, Page. I have extended the offer, but I'm not sure if she thought it was in jest or not."

He smiled at her. "She has a very special place for you in her heart."

"But will it be enough to draw her from her family and the only home she's ever known?"

"Time will tell, but I'd be surprised if she was left behind."

"I can only hope you're right."

They gazed across the unusually calm ocean, the surface almost glasslike, reflecting the light of the newly risen moon. "I suspect that some of the slave ships come from Norfolk. Let's keep an eye open when we're in port to see if we can determine the size of their crew and the number of slaves they transport. If there are too many, I don't think even my conscience will agree to an attempted rescue."

"If we are successful, where do you plan to take them?"

"I've found a couple of locations on the islands south, off the coast of La Florida. I think we could release them there, that would provide enough distance to keep them safe."

"Very well, my captain. I think I'll turn in and hope for another day of swift winds. My tolerance of stew has met its match, and I'm ready for a hearty meal in port."

"That we shall have, my friend. Rest well, and I'll see you in the morning."

"Goodnight Captain."

†

Hillary leaned back against the bale where she and Cecelia had made love, and a hundred butterflies took flight in her stomach. Her plans to retire included Cecelia, but if

Cecelia refused to accompany her, Hillary would make do on her tiny slice of heaven in the islands.

Her thoughts wandered from Cecelia, to the mass of slaves housed in the small barracoon. The image of their misery was etched in her mind, and though she would contribute to freeing only a small number, at least that many would run to freedom. Her eyes grew heavy, and as the ship shifted from a swell, her head snapped up. She climbed down from the bales and retired to her comfortable bed.

†

The next evening, as darkness fell, they dropped anchor within sight of Norfolk. The few lights of the city glowed gently on the horizon. Early the next morning, they would approach the harbor and the docking slip allocated to her ship.

She spoke to the men that evening. After minor hesitation, all agreed to her plans. As Page had predicted, her married sailors also wished to participate, but she flatly refused. With gentle prodding, she explained the potential perils to their families.

She paced the deck nervously, as she mentally reviewed her plans for rescuing the captive souls. The risk was high, but with careful execution, she felt certain her plan would succeed. When she retired to bed, she was plagued with dreams. Men carrying torches dragged her and her crew to the giant oak in the center of Savannah, the hanging tree. She woke to a cold sweat covering her body, and realizing it for a dream, dove swiftly into the dark waters of sleep.

†

Ringing church bells welcomed her on deck, as the crew pulled up anchor and raised enough sail to get them safely into the harbor. As she pulled into her assigned slip to unload, she noticed a cumbersome looking ship moored beside her. The planks of her decking were ill kept, and the hull looked marginally seaworthy, signs of a captain more interested in the weight of his purse than the upkeep of his ship. She wasn't surprised to see the crew loading crates of goods, nor the small group of chained slaves massed tightly together, the next cargo to be loaded. She counted twenty, mostly women and children, in the group. The women and children were easier to control than strong, young men, and would be forced into the fields to pick cotton. Young children clung to their mothers unchained. The heavy, steel cuffs were too large for their small arms, and they were unlikely to leave the protection of their mothers and older siblings. Hillary sent up a silent prayer that those men would burn in hell for the plight of these enslaved people.

With the ship securely moored, Hillary turned to Page. "You are in command here. Keep an eye on the number of crew boarding the ship next to us," she whispered. "I'll be back as soon as I can." She stepped off the ship and started down the dock. As she passed the small cluster of slaves, the overseer cracked his whip to keep the group's attention on him instead of the beautiful young woman walking away from him. She flinched at the crack of the whip but was relieved it struck only air and not human flesh. *At least for now. Morgan, that's your name, you worthless bastard.*

As she walked deeper into town, she saw a small crowd milling about a center courtyard, where another group of slaves was gathered. She stopped at the crack of the whip that brought these slaves to their feet. The auctioneer took his place on a roughly made wooden platform. She was about to turn away from the group, when an older couple caught her eye. They were fully dressed in relatively clean clothing and seemed out of place. The woman clung dearly to the man, who Hillary surmised was her husband. They took tentative steps onto the wooden platform.

"This pair, a married couple, has served their master until his death. Too old for field work, this fine couple would make an excellent addition to any number of fine households in the area," the auctioneer explained. "Who will open the bid for these fine specimens?"

The crowd was silent. Apparently, no one was in the market for house slaves. Hillary did not intend to become a slave owner, but something about the couple called to her heart.

"Let's move on to the field hands," an angry voice shouted from the crowd.

"I'll give you five dollars for the pair."

"Five dollars is a steal for this fine pair, do I have another offer?" The auctioneer pleaded for another bid. When none came, he struck his gavel on the wooden table and called "sold."

"Good, now let's get on with it," another voice shouted from the crowd.

Hillary had just become a slave owner. She cringed at the thought, but she knew she would give them their freedom once they were in a safe location. She walked to the purser's table and paid for the couple. She took the papers of ownership transfer and tucked them into her pocket, as the couple was delivered to her. As the slaves were released from their shackles, Hillary watched them rub their chafed wrists.

Neither looked up at Hilary. "My name is Captain Hillary Blythe, and I hope neither of you gets seasick. Come, we need to pick up some supplies, and then we will return to my ship. What are your names?"

The man raised his head to look up at her. "I am Joseph Smith, and this is my wife, Mary."

"I sure hope one of you can cook, because my crew makes terrible meals."

"Oh yes'm," Mary said. "Master says I'm an excellent cook. I've cooked for Master Benson for more than twenty years."

"What happened to him?"

"He took ill with consumption, and his son wanted everything sold off after his death," Joseph explained.

"Mary, I'll need you to decide on supplies to feed a crew of eight for breakfast and supper. Also, plan on a large portion of oats." If the rescue of slaves were successful, a hearty portion of oatmeal with plenty of sugar would go a long way in sustaining a large group.

"Yes ma'am, I'll be glad to do that, Captain."

"Fine, do you have any special skills, Joseph?"

"I was a houseman for Master Benson, but I can be taught many things. I'm a good learner."

"You've done well with learning English. Do you still speak your native tongue?"

"Only in the privacy of our quarters. We are allowed to speak only English to Master."

"Well, let's get a move on, so we can make it back to the ship."

Joseph picked up two small bags holding their belongings, and they followed her to the general store. Mary went to work selecting food supplies, which Joseph carried to the merchant's counter. Hillary selected two pistols, powder and loads, as well as several bolts of colored cloth to trade in the islands. The women loved the colorful cotton material. They would barter foods, jewelry, and other goods, for the fabric.

Joseph helped the shop owner load the purchases into a large pushcart. The store's delivery boy would push the cart to the ship and help them unload before returning. Hillary paid for the supplies and led the small group back to the ship.

†

Page looked at Hillary with a quizzical look when the couple followed her onboard carrying supplies.

"I'll explain in just a bit. Let me get our supplies settled." Hillary led them into the galley and showed them where the goods could be stored. There was a small private room off the galley, they could use as their quarters. "It's not much, but it will give you some privacy."

"It will do just fine, Captain." Mary gave her a bashful smile. "Do you think we could buy a few more cooking supplies before we leave?" Her eyes surveyed the small galley.

"Anything that will help you cook delicious meals." Hillary chuckled. "Can you make a list and we'll go back to the general store?"

"I can, Captain," Joseph replied. "My Mary doesn't read or write."

36

"We will stay here for the night and set sail in the morning. I promised the crew a hearty meal in port tonight. You will join us of course."

Joseph's eyes left hers. "No ma'am, we are not allowed."

"What?" She realized there was so much she didn't know. "Come sit with me." She sat and they joined her at the table. "I have never been a slave owner and don't intend to start now." She saw Mary's eyes fill with fear as she looked to her husband. "As soon as I figure out what is best, your freedom will be restored. I will not hold you as slaves. You are now members of our crew."

Hillary watched Joseph smile with relief, no longer fearing being sold once again. "Thank you, Captain. We will work hard for you." He wrapped his arm around Mary who had started to cry.

"I'll give you time to get settled in. If there are personal supplies like clothing, shoes or other items you need, please add them to the list." Hillary saw him nod, and she left the galley to walk back on deck.

"Welcome back, Captain."

"Thanks, Page."

He smirked. "So, you're a slave owner now?"

"I'll have you know, they will be free as soon as we depart this port. I couldn't stand to see what would happen to these two in the auction blocks. No one wanted older house slaves, so I bid. I think they will be very helpful on the ship, and we'll finally have a decent cook."

"Well, that in itself is a blessing. I'm absolutely sick of pirate stew."

She smiled back at him. "Me too. What have you discovered today?"

"A group of twenty slaves, the ones you saw amassed earlier. Mostly women and children, and a crew of three, just as you suggested. They've taken them down to the hold and will be departing soon."

"That sounds like good odds."

"Are you concerned about them leaving tonight, while we're still in port?"

"No, we can easily overtake them before they reach Savannah or Charleston. Have you studied the condition of his ship? It's slow and poorly kempt."

"That's very true. I'm amazed it even holds its own in port." Page rubbed his forehead. "You know, I have an ache in my bones."

"Your bad weather headache?"

"Yes, that's the one. I'm glad we won't be taking on a full cargo, so we can travel fast and light."

"We'll head to deeper waters, if the weather becomes too rough."

"I know we'll be in good hands. You know these waters better than anyone." He smiled his confidence in her skills. "Fish, or a nice steak tonight, Captain?"

She pondered his question. "I think maybe a bit of both, Page."

"Now you're singing my tune. Good idea, Captain."

"How much longer until we're loaded?"

"Maybe an hour. Then we'll relax until we go to supper."

"Very good. I've got another run to the general store for some kitchen supplies, but I'll be joining the men for supper."

"What are the names of our new crew members?"

"Mary and Joseph Smith."

"Mary and Joseph? Are you serious?"

"You know slave owners aren't real creative in naming their slaves. These are somewhat educated and speak in both English and their native tongue."

"That could be useful when we overtake the slave ship, to have someone communicate what we are doing."

"My thoughts exactly." Their conversation ended when Joseph came on deck with his list.

He handed her the list. "This is what Mary says she'll need to better the galley, Captain."

Hillary reviewed the list. "Not as bad as I feared." She smiled. "Are you ready to go make our purchases?"

He smiled. "Yes, Captain."

She nodded to Page. "This is Mr. Page, my first mate and the man in charge when I'm not onboard."

"Mr. Page." He nodded.

"Welcome aboard, Joseph, I am pleased to hear Mary is a good cook."

Joseph looked up and smiled. "Oh, yes sir, she's a wonderful cook."

"Let's get her set up with a proper galley. See you soon, Page."

✝

When they returned from the store, Mary marveled at the new cooking implements as if they were Christmas presents. Hillary had also purchased additional bacon, ham, and other cured meats. She was surprised that neither of them had asked for anything for personal use. She had questioned Joseph, but he assured her they had what they needed.

"What would you like for supper, Captain?" Mary asked, as she stored the supplies.

"Remember, I will be taking the crew on shore for supper tonight. You just have to cook for the two of you. Come sit with me a few minutes, and then you can finish."

Once seated around the table, Hillary explained her plan to them. They were delighted to hear again her proposal for giving them their freedom, but Mary's eyes grew wide when Hillary told her about her strategy to rescue others."

"You knows you'll hang if you caught freeing slaves, Captain."

"I know Mary, but I'm willing to take some risk to right this horrible wrong. I will need help from you and Joseph to assist with communication, if our plan works."

"We will aid in any way we can," Joseph assured her.

"That's all I can ask. We won't be late tonight. We'll be underway at first light and will break for a meal after we reach clear water."

"I'll be ready with a meal. Do you drink coffee, Captain?"

"With plenty of sugar and sweet milk when we have it."

"I'll send Joseph up with a mug when we leave the port," Mary promised.

"That would be good. I'll check in on you when we return."

"Thank you for everything, Captain. We will work very hard for you," Joseph said.

"I'm sure you will. Once we get out to sea, report to Mr. Page. He'll start teaching you to be a sailor."

"Yes, Captain." Joseph's smile lit the room.

"I don't feel it's necessary to say this, but don't leave the ship tonight. I don't want anyone to take you for runaways," she warned.

"We know the risks, and we promise not to step foot ashore without you." Joseph smiled up at her.

Hillary nodded and returned to the deck. Page was relaxing against the railing, as he stared across open water.

"Are you ready for some good food?"

He turned to face her, and she saw the worry on his face. "Yes, Captain, I am."

"Are you having second thoughts?"

"No, just worried about the weather."

"We've seen our share of bad weather. Are you more worried than usual?"

He grinned. "No more than usual, Captain. I'm sure we'll fare well."

"Let's go eat. If tomorrow dawns and you feel uneasy, we can stay in port. I trust your bones." She chuckled and slapped him on the shoulder.

†

Hillary walked the deck the next morning and looked across the horizon. *Red skies at night, sailor's delight. Red skies at morning, sailors take warning.* Page's ominous feeling was seeping into her body, and she shivered in the cool morning. *Most storms this time of year come from the south. Do we try to run through it, or wait it out?*

Page joined her on deck. "What do you think, Captain?"

"How do your bones feel? I'm not liking the color of that sky."

41

"My bones are still aching, but not as bad."

"How would you feel about eating a nice breakfast and waiting to see what the day brings? We could leave by afternoon and still make good time before nightfall."

"I wouldn't argue with a good breakfast and a few hours delay. I'm sure the men wouldn't either. It will give us time to get to know Mary and Joseph too."

"That it would Mr. Page. Go ask Mary to start cooking and inform the crew of our delay."

Page nodded. "Very well, Captain."

Hillary was still staring out at the horizon when Joseph walked up beside her.

"The sky looks angry, doesn't it?"

She turned and took the mug of coffee he offered. "Yes it does, Joseph. We're going to stay in port for a bit, to see what develops."

"That's what Mr. Page just told us. Mary will have breakfast ready soon. Do you want me to come and get you?"

"No Joseph, I can't change the weather by staring at the sky. I'll go down with you."

As expected, Mary had cooked a delicious breakfast. During the meal, Joseph shared with the crew how they had become slaves. Stolen from two different villages in Africa, he and Mary met on the ship that carried them to America. They fell in love and posed as a married couple when they arrived. Thankfully, their Master Benson purchased them as a pair. Several years later, they performed the rite of jumping the broom, when Master Benson was off on a trip. Unfortunately, they were never blessed with children. Just as well, since they would have been born into slavery. The crew listened intently to their story.

"Do you remember your tribal names?" Page asked.

Joseph hung his head. "We can still speak our native tongues, but our original names have been lost over the years. We became Joseph and Mary Smith, and that was all that mattered."

"That is still all that matters. I was just curious." Page smiled at the couple. "That was a wonderful meal, Mary. I'm so glad we don't have to suffer through our own stew any longer."

"I love to cook, and I like to see hearty appetites appreciate my cooking."

Hillary responded with a chuckle. "That will not be a problem aboard this ship." She poured another mug of coffee and excused herself to walk on deck.

Page rose to join her.

When they emerged, they saw dark thunderheads growing in the north. Flecks of sunlight broke through the clouds in the south. She looked at Page. "What do you think? Make a break for it and run through or wait and ride it out?"

"Obviously, I'm no better at waiting than you are. Let's make a run for it. We have a slave ship to catch up to anyhow."

"Get the crew started, and let's run to the south." She grinned back at him.

Hillary watched Page explain the workings of the crew to Joseph. Large white sails were raised after the mooring lines were unfastened, and Page barked orders to shift the sails to allow the wind to carry them from the harbor. Joseph listened intently, as Page explained what the crew was doing. He laughed as the young lookout, Manu, scurried up the netting to the crow's nest.

"He's like a spider climbing up a web," Joseph said.

"More like a monkey on a vine," Page answered with a hearty laugh. "He's got very sharp eyes, though, and will warn us of dangers we cannot see from deck level."

The winds were swift, and it did not take long for the ship to clear the harbor. Open water lay ahead, the swells creating a chop, as the ship plunged forward. An hour out of the harbor, the seas calmed, but rain began to fall. In the crow's nest, Manu donned a tarp and used the brim of his hat and his hand to keep the rain from blurring his vision.

Page, had gone below deck and returned wearing an oilskin coat that would repel water. "I'll take the wheel for a few hours while you dry out, then we can switch."

Hillary allowed him to take the helm and disappeared into the galley. "Please, tell me you still have some coffee, Mary?" She took a seat at the table and shivered.

"I do, Captain. Joseph, bring a warm blanket."

Mary filled a mug with coffee, sugar, and sweet milk, and carried it to Hillary. "Thanks, Mary." Hillary took a long sip from the warming liquid, as Joseph draped a blanket across her shoulders. The aroma of cooking food reached her nostrils, as she attempted to warm. "Whatever that is you have cooking sure smells good."

"I'm baking some cornbread, to go with fresh greens, and I'll fry up some chops later. Are you hungry? I still have ham left from breakfast and some fresh bread."

"I wasn't hungry until I came in here." Hillary looked at Mary. "I'd love a ham sandwich."

She watched Mary's body swaying with the motion of the ship. "You seem to be adapting well to being onboard. Does your stomach feel okay?"

"I was a bit ill at first, but I chewed some mint leaf. It helped my stomach settle down. Would you care for a slice of cheese?"

"That would be perfect." Hillary shrugged off the blanket and took the sandwich. "I know it's not lush accommodations, but did you rest well last night?"

"It was the best night's sleep we had since Master Benson passed away," Joseph replied. "We fared just fine, Captain."

Hillary pondered her thoughts, as she chewed the delicious sandwich. "What do you wish of your future?"

Joseph looked at Mary, who nodded to him. "We'd like to serve aboard your ship for as long as you'd have us. We have no place to go, and this seems a safe place for us."

"We are headed to Cuba and then on to the islands of the Caribbean. We'll take on supplies for Boston. After that, we'll head back to Savannah for a load of cotton to take to Norfolk, to complete our cycle. You are welcome to stay aboard as long as you wish."

†

When she took over the helm, Page placed the coat over her shoulders. The rain was slowing, but the low-hanging clouds meant it would pick up once more. She did not regret the decision to leave the safety of the port. So far, they had not encountered anything worse than heavy rains. But that was not to continue.

The winds and waves picked up by late afternoon, and the sun failed to peek through the heavy clouds. Hillary was ready to locate a deep cove and drop anchor, when Manu called from the crow's nest.

"A ship has crashed into a reef, Captain." He called down and pointed to the direction.

She gazed out through sheets of rain, across the choppy waters. The dark, massive form of the slave ship appeared. *This couldn't be any more perfect. If only we're not too late.*

Page stepped on deck and handed Hillary a spyglass. She extended the lens and looked at the ship, listing sideways as it took on water. Three hundred yards toward shore, she saw a rowboat, carrying the three crew members. They had abandoned ship and left their human cargo to drown. She tossed the spyglass to Page. "We have to hurry. I just pray we aren't already too late. Rouse the crew and ask Mary to start cooking a large pot of oats."

Hillary spun the wheel to the right with the intentions of bringing her ship as close to the wrecked ship as possible. She prayed the waves would relent and allow her to attempt a rescue without jeopardizing her own crew and ship. When Page returned, she explained her plan to him, as the increasing waves slammed into the side of their ship.

"I'll pull us along as close as I can, but we'll need to use the netting to get them to safety on our ship. Someone from our ship will need to board and secure the netting. I'll stay at the helm and keep us as steady as possible," Hillary said.

"I'll board first," Manu volunteered, after coming down from his post. "I seem to be the most agile of the crew." He grinned.

"Grab the loaded pistols, Page. The crew has abandoned ship, but you need to be prepared just in case. Bring mine along as well." She turned to Joseph. "You will need to accompany Mr. Page and explain to the captives what is going on."

"Yes, Captain." He nodded, eager to be a part of the plan. He waited at the side of the ship as they drew close, anxious to get on board.

Hillary struggled at the helm to hold the ship into position. Her arms were already aching from exertion, but the adrenalin pumping through her veins gave her the strength she needed.

The crew moved to the side of the ship after gathering the netting. Page returned with the pistols. "I don't think this would be considered piracy, since they've abandoned ship and left their cargo to die," he said.

"You're right on that account, but releasing them to freedom will be, I'm afraid."

"We can worry about that later. Let's get them safely aboard first."

As soon as she had drawn close, Manu jumped across and scurried up the side of the ship. He caught the edge of the netting and secured it to the sinking ship. "We have to hurry," he called back. "There's a large gash in the hull and she's taking on water quickly."

"Good luck," she said to Page, and watched her crew board the ship. With every new wave, Hillary could hear wood splintering, as the ship was torn apart by the angry ocean. Her crew would have to act quickly or risk their ship being dragged down with the wreck.

She watched Page open the entrance to the cargo hold. Joseph and Manu entered first.

The stench of human waste assaulted them as soon as they entered. Even with the hull breached, the heat contained in the cargo hold was viscous. Several pairs of terrified eyes looked up at them through the darkness. Page shouted over the wind, "Tell them what is going on, Joseph."

Joseph spoke softly, his words easing the terror of the group, as they stood and moved toward the men. Page and Manu began hauling out the slaves, soaked to the bone. The children wailed in fear of the horrific, raging storm that slammed the ships together with the arrival of each new wave. The crew stationed themselves to help the captives traverse the netting, catching several as they lost their grips on the wet ropes. Their efforts prevented the rescued slaves from falling to certain death, crushed between two ships in the raging ocean.

✝

Hillary watched as they cleared the netting and stepped safely aboard her ship. Mary had come from the galley and was leading them into the small, dry cargo hold. She spoke in a language only they understood. Hillary was grateful for buying Mary and Joseph their freedom and for their ability to communicate with these frightened, tortured souls.

She breathed a sigh of relief when the crew climbed back on deck. She counted heads to make sure they had all returned safely. "All accounted for."

She saw the pained look on Page's face. "Not quite," he said. "Two of the children drowned."

"We did the best we could," she tried to console him. "Send Manu back into the crow's nest. I'd like to put in a few miles before we shelter for the night. There should be a secluded cove about five miles ahead."

48

Page spoke briefly with Manu, who scrambled into the crow's nest, then he went below deck to check on the new arrivals. Several of the crew were already using tools to break the shackles free from the captives. He sent Mary and Joseph back to the galley to bring the hot oats.

Joseph stopped by the helm on his way.

"Do they understand what is happening?" she asked.

"Yes, Captain they do. They send thanks and prayers for their rescue."

"Good, let's get some food into them. Get them free of those damned chains and tucked away safely for the night."

Joseph nodded, then went below to help Mary.

Hillary gave orders to reposition the sails, and they broke free from the rapidly disappearing slave ship. She peered across the water, but could no longer see the rowboat. *Hopefully, those bastards drowned.* If I can't see them, they probably can't see us. She steered the boat toward open waters and away from the treacherous reefs. She heard the slave ship break in two and watched as the mast fell below the waves. She let out a sigh of relief when the last fingers of rock slipped out of her view, and she focused on the dark waters ahead.

An hour later, Manu called out. She circled the small cove so the ship faced the ocean, and ordered the anchor dropped. The harrowing night at sea was ending. Joseph informed her the crew's dinner would be ready shortly, but she wanted to check on her passengers before sitting down to a hot meal.

Page and Manu had taken over the task of freeing the chains, and she couldn't help but smile at the growing pile of steel tossed in the corner. She would enjoy dropping them in the ocean once they were underway again tomorrow. They would never again be used to cause misery and pain.

Dark eyes watched her approach. The passengers were using their fingers to eat the sugared oatmeal. She hadn't planned on extra bowls and spoons, but they ate hungrily, appearing to do quite well with their fingers. A young girl of around eight years old smiled up at her, and offered her some food. Hillary smiled back and gestured for the girl to continue eating, warmed by the generosity of the child.

Page struck a blow near a woman's wrist and angrily tossed the final shackle into the pile.

"Don't we still have some old sail cloth stored down here?" she asked. "That could provide them a bit of warmth as they huddle together."

"Yes, Captain, I believe we do."

She and Page located the tattered sail and draped it around the group. "I think that's the best we can do for now. Send one of the crew down with a jug of fresh water, and I'll meet you in the galley."

She walked to her quarters for fresh clothing, then joined her crew. Every one of them wore a smile, as she sat at the table. "I'm very proud of you all, and I hope you realize how important and wonderful tonight's events are. You've saved a small group from a lifetime of misery and abuse."

"Indeed we have, Captain. Thanks to you," Page said, as he lifted his mug. "To freedom."

"Hear, hear," the crew chanted.

They enjoyed a much-deserved hot meal in relative silence. After the meal, Hillary retired to her quarters and fell into an exhausted sleep.

CHAPTER THREE

Morning dawned on a glorious day. The skies were a beautiful, crystal blue, and the winds were strong. After breakfast, Hillary got the ship underway, as Joseph and Mary fed the passengers more of the sugary oatmeal.

"What do we do with them now?" Page asked, as he stood beside her at the helm.

"I remembered, this morning, that about eight days south is a Christian mission on one of the islands, right near the ocean. Antigua is the name. We've picked up goods there before. I bet they will take on the settling of these freed slaves. A few pieces of silver may help to influence the decision."

"If not? What then?"

"We take them farther on to the islands with us. Cuba is not a possibility. They would end up forced back into slavery there, but I'm sure one of the other islands will accept them kindly. Until then, pray for fast winds and that our oats hold out. We cannot chance going into port to resupply with this cargo."

"I'm sure Manu and a few of the men wouldn't mind an opportunity to do some fishing. Once we settle for the night, he can use that cast net of his to see what he can catch."

"That's a great idea, Page. See what you can get set up. Also, ask Mary and Joseph to start bringing small groups on deck to stretch their legs. If another ship comes in sight, they must go below to avoid detection."

"Yes, Captain." He nodded and grinned before walking into the galley.

When Page returned, Hillary turned to him. "Will you and Joseph bring that pile of shackles out to the deck and bring several of the women up with you?"

He looked at her curiously but followed her instruction. When he and Joseph carried the last of the shackles and chains onto the deck, the two mothers who lost their children and another woman followed them. "Please, ask them to heave those chains as far as they can into the ocean, so no others will be bound by them."

Joseph beamed a smile at her. "With pleasure, Captain."

He talked to the women for several minutes, then took up a length of chain. He hurled it as far as he could. The women smiled and took great pleasure in disposing of the source of so much pain and misery. The crew cheered when the last set of shackles disappeared beneath the waves.

†

Hillary smiled when the lighthouse at Tybee Island came into view, and she blew a kiss across the wind to Cecelia. *I will be back soon for you, my love.*

The fishing gods smiled down on Manu. With the help of his mates, he managed to catch and land a large tuna, which kept them all fed through four days of travel, extending the oats to only a breakfast meal.

When they reached Antigua, she guided the ship toward the small mission. Hillary and Page used the rowboat to go ashore. Hillary was pleased. She didn't even have to bribe the Methodist missionary to take on her passengers. She scowled at George, an overseer of one of the large plantations, who rushed to her in hopes he could convince her to sell the slaves to him. She assured him that she would never sell another human into slavery. She smiled at Elizabeth Allen, who gladly accepted them into her flock with a promise to teach them the language and the ways of Christians. Hillary placed four silver pieces in Elizabeth's hand as a gesture of thanks, before she returned to the ship. Manu and Joseph ferried the freed slaves to the island. Joseph explained to the group what was happening, and he was pleased to find a man waiting on the beach who could speak their language. Once they were all safely ashore, the tiny group gathered at the beach and waved as the ship continued its southern journey.

"That worked out well," Page said, as he took up his post beside her.

"Yes, it did, but I'll be honest. I'm not cut out to be a pirate."

"Me either, Captain, but if we run across another abandoned slave ship, we know exactly what to do."

"That we do, Page. That we do."

†

They traveled on to Cuba and delivered the sweet Virginian tobacco. Hillary received a wooden box filled with Cuban cigars for her timely delivery. She had tasted her first smoke on their last voyage and fallen in love with cigars. She would smoke the cherished gift sparingly to make them stretch. The trip down to the islands went perfectly, and after a day's rest and resupplying, they departed for Boston. They passed the small plantation Hillary had purchased on Saint Lucia and pulled into the harbor for a quick visit. Juan, the man hired to run the business for her, met her on the docks with a warm smile and a cool drink.

"Will you be staying with us for a while?"

"No Juan, not this trip. Soon, I'll retire and you can teach me all about farming."

"I look forward to that." He smiled. "Will you and your crew at least join us for some lunch?"

"That we can do. Let us tidy up here, and we'll be on our way."

†

Juan led the crew on a tour of the plantation and described the various crops grown on the island, mainly bananas, pineapples, coconuts, and sugar cane.

"I'm wondering if tobacco could grow here, Juan."

"Years ago, it was grown here, until sugar cane became more profitable. If you bring some seeds, we can give it a try."

54

Page chuckled. "You could learn to roll your own cigars then," he teased.

"That I could." She smiled back at her first mate.

They dined on smoked fish and fresh island vegetables, and drank a tea sweetened with coconut milk. "I could grow fat here eating meals like this every day," Page groaned, as he pushed his plate away.

"We would work you so hard you'd never have to worry about gaining weight," Juan promised him.

Page looked around at the beautiful water, white sandy beaches, and the mountains in the distance. "It would be a temptation hard to resist. Maybe in a few years, I can afford a spot close to you," he aimed at Hillary.

"If we can make tobacco and coffee beans work, that may provide another option for delivery to America."

"That is very true, Captain. Something worth thinking about."

Juan's interest was piqued. "There is a spot not far from here that may become available soon."

Page's eyes lit up.

"I'll keep an eye on it, and if possible, purchase it for you," Hillary said. "You can always sell the ship and delivery contacts."

"That's true."

"If we are to make any money on this trip, we'd better be going," she told them. "I'll be seeing you soon, Juan. Thank you for a lovely meal."

"My pleasure, Captain. Safe travels, and hurry back to us."

As the sails raised, Hillary glanced back at the place she would soon make her home, and smiled. All she had to do was convince Cecelia to come spend her life with her."

†

The wind was plentiful, and the weather held for their return to Boston. Mary and Joseph accompanied Hillary into the city, to order food and supplies. The clerk at the general store was a well-dressed black man, who had bought his freedom and traveled north to start a new life. Mary and Joseph talked with him, while Hillary placed her order. She saw the shine in their eyes when they left the store.

They stopped off at a small coffee house, and she bought them an early lunch. Joseph's eyes still shone with the excitement of seeing black people moving freely about the city. "This wouldn't be a bad place for you to start a new life, if that's what you wanted."

Joseph's head snapped back to her. "This seems to be a nice place, but Mary and I have another idea, if you're willing."

Hillary smiled at him. "I'm listening."

"We had a small garden where we grew vegetables for Master Benson. We'd like to stay with you on the island, when you retire, and help out there."

Hillary's eyes grew wide. "I'd like that very much. I do pay staff there, but it won't make you rich by any means."

"You've already made us rich by giving us our freedom. Keep us fed, a roof over our heads, and we'll work for you to the day we move on from this world."

"Mr. and Mrs. Smith, you have yourselves a deal." Hillary offered him her hand, and he gladly shook it.

Everything seemed to be falling into place. If she could convince Cecelia to join her, they would make the deliveries to Norfolk and Cuba, then sail to their new home.

†

When they arrived back in Savannah, Hillary and Page walked to the DuPont chandlery. "Please, supervise the unloading at the docks, while I see if I can talk privately with Cecelia, to tell her of my plans."

"Consider it done, Captain. I'll also find out if they are ready with a shipment of cotton. I think we are a day or so ahead of our normal schedule."

"If not, that only gives me more time to convince Cecelia."

Page noted the look of worry on her face. "Everything will work out as planned."

"I sure hope you're right. If not, I'm still determined to move on with life. I'd just prefer she were a part of it."

"I understand."

Cecil's head popped up when they entered the office at the DuPont chandlery. "Captain, Mr. Page, I'm glad to see you. You've made it ahead of schedule again." He smiled.

"The winds pushing us south were quite fair. I hope an early arrival does not disrupt your schedule." Hillary's eyes searched for Cecelia.

"Absolutely not for the delivery, but I'm afraid the last of the cotton bales won't arrive until late tomorrow. That will delay your departure."

"I'm sure the crew won't mind an extra day to relax in your beautiful city," she answered. "We've been out to sea a fair amount lately. We could all use a bit of a rest."

"I feel I must warn you then, Cecelia has other plans for you. She has rented a buggy and plans to take you over to

Tybee for the day." He chuckled. "You know, once she sets her mind to something, she won't be stopped."

"That sounds like the perfect way to spend a relaxing day. Where is the fair maiden?"

"She went home to bring our lunch and should be back shortly. You can have your men deliver the cargo this afternoon. Send a few men up, and they can drive the wagons down to your ship."

"I will do that, sir. Please, tell Cecelia I will see her this afternoon."

"Indeed, and I'm sure I will see you this afternoon, as well."

"We will take a meal of our own, and I'll send the men up for the wagons."

†

"Miss Cecelia's plan for a day at the beach sounds like the perfect opportunity for you to have a private conversation with her."

"Yes, that seems to have worked out perfectly, Page."

They returned to the ship, and she sent Page to give the crew orders. Hillary entered the galley to find Mary busy cooking a meal. "I should have known you would already be cooking." She smiled. Joseph was sitting at the table, working out a list of food supplies they needed. "We can go to the general store after our meal. Be warned. You are not to stray from the ship without the company of myself or Mr. Page." She sighed. "Savannah is much like Norfolk in its treatment of Africans. They may take you for runaways."

"Yes, Captain. We would never consider going ashore without you."

58

"We will be in port for two days, while we wait on the arrival of our next shipment. We will have some time to relax."

"I'd like to do a bit of sewing then, if you would be so kind as to purchase some fabric. Joseph's shirts and my dresses are looking worn," Mary requested.

"You can pick out whatever fabric and supplies you need," Hillary assured her.

"The chowder and sandwiches are ready, Joseph. Would you bring in the crew?" Mary asked her husband.

"That sure does smell good." Hillary sniffed the air.

Mary smiled warmly at her. "Have a seat, good Captain, and I'll have a bowl for you in a hurry."

†

When they returned to the DuPont chandlery, later in the afternoon, Hillary smiled as they passed the empty barracoon. "It's good to see that spot vacant. I'm sure our previous passengers would have been held there for days."

"Yes it is, Captain," Page agreed.

Cecelia was in the warehouse when they arrived, preparing to take inventory of the cargo-filled wagons, which would arrive from the ship shortly. She looked up at the sound of their approach. "Good afternoon, Captain, Mr. Page. Nice to see you both again."

"Likewise, Miss Cecelia." He smiled.

"I'm so happy to see you both. I have been worried ever since we got word of the tragedy." Deep lines marred Cecelia's forehead.

"What tragedy?" Hillary asked with concern.

"A ship carrying twenty slaves wrecked and sunk during a devastating storm, drowning the human cargo." Tears welled in her eyes.

Hillary feigned surprise. "That is tragic. What of the crew?"

"They barely managed to escape with their lives before the ship sank. They rowed ashore and made their way to Charleston," Cecelia reported.

"Yes, we ran into some of that weather. It was treacherous for a while, but we were able to find safety in a secluded cove."

"I just feel so terrible, for those people to die like that, chained so they didn't even have a chance to survive," Cecelia said, the tears on the verge of falling.

"There's a special place in hell for the men who left them to die like that," Hillary promised.

"I hope you're right. That Captain and his crew are trying to arrange for a new ship, so they can continue the business. That cruel overseer, Morgan, has been in town all week, making proposals to buy a ship."

"Hopefully, they will be a long time in getting one," Page chuckled.

"We can only hope," Hillary agreed. "What they did is beyond belief."

The first wagon arrived, interrupting their conversation. "I understand we have a trip planned for tomorrow."

"Yes, I wasn't sure of your arrival, so I just need to make preparations for a meal, and we'll be set." Cecelia spoke with a light blush to her cheeks. "I hope you don't mind."

"Not at all. What a perfect way to spend a day, with a beautiful woman at the beach."

Cecelia smiled. "I'm so looking forward to it."

"As am I. I will take care of the meal, so don't fret over that. We have a wonderful new cook onboard. You will enjoy her food"

"Will you join us for dinner tonight? Mother is eager to meet you. Father and I have told her so many stories about you."

They may regret that, when I steal their only daughter away from them. "I'd be honored. What time should I arrive?"

"Dinner is promptly at seven." Cecelia smiled.

"I shall see you at seven then," Hillary replied and returned to her ship.

†

She spied the box of Cuban cigars and decided it would be polite to share one with Cecil after dinner. I'm afraid her mother would disapprove of a woman smoking, so I'll refrain. Maybe I'll have one after I return.

Mary sat at the galley table, sewing a new shirt for Joseph. "I have a dinner engagement for tonight, but I wonder if, tomorrow, you would put together a picnic meal for two."

"I would, indeed. Do you know what you would like?"

"I'll leave that up to you, Mary."

"I should think some fruit and the new cheese we bought today. I'm cooking fried chicken for the men tonight, so I'll set some aside. Do you have a bottle of Madeira?"

"Excellent idea, I'll go buy some right now. Is there anything else you need?"

"A picnic basket or crate would work wonders." Mary smiled.

"Yes, I could see where that would help. I'll see what I can do. Thank you, Mary."

✝

Hillary walked to the opposite end of town to buy the wine. Near the entrance to the shop, she lucked into a nice wooden crate with handles, used to deliver wine. "This will do nicely." She hefted the crate to check its sturdiness. The clerk chuckled at her offer to buy it and ended up tossing it in for free.

She returned with the crate, and Mary lined it with some of the torn sail cloth they had used to cover the freed slaves. "That will do just fine." She nestled the bottle of wine and two mugs into the crate.

Hillary walked back to her cabin and began pacing nervously, anxious about her dinner at the DuPont home. Her eyes landed on the box of cigars. *Maybe better now than later, to calm my nerves.* She selected two of the treasured treats and went in search of Page.

She found him on deck, supervising the loading of the last of the cargo to be delivered to the DuPont chandlery. "Would you care to join me for a smoke?" She knew that Page generally preferred to smoke a pipe, but the cigars were a relished treat.

"Are we celebrating something special?"

"No, just calming my nerves before my dinner at the DuPont's."

62

Page smirked. "Her mother sounds like she could be formidable."

"I said calm my nerves not set them further on edge," she growled. "Do you have a light?"

Page took the cigars and disappeared inside the galley, where he used the oil candle's flame to light the cigars. He handed Hillary a lit cigar when he returned. "Let's go find a spot to sit." He walked with her down the loading plank to a low, stone wall. They took a seat and stretched out their legs. "Now, this is heavenly," he said, as he blew out the sweet smoke. "I hope you were serious about me becoming your neighbor in the islands."

"I couldn't think of anyone I'd enjoy more as a neighbor."

"Just a week or so, and you'll be an official islander. Are you ready for life on land?"

Hillary's eyes landed on the sturdy wooden hull and strong sails of her small vessel that had seen her safely through many months at sea. "She's been a good ship, but I'm ready to put down some roots. I can't think of a more beautiful place to live."

"I'll agree with you there. Do you think we could use the ship to transport the goods we grow?"

"It's possible. Especially, if we have two plantations working together. Alone, I don't think I'd produce that much, but it's something to consider. Even if it's only island hopping to barter goods. I'd like to purchase some seeds while we're in Norfolk," Hilary added. "Once I arrive on the island, I'll buy some livestock, some chickens, and some hogs, to keep us supplied in meat. Mary and Joseph are excited to plant a garden spot for vegetables."

"So, they've decided to stay with you?"

"Yes. They've got no place else to call home, and Mary is such a good cook."

"Don't remind me," Page said. "It'll be back to pirate stew for us, unless I can find a decent replacement."

"Maybe that cute little red-haired girl you visit in Norfolk?" Hillary suggested.

Page surprised her by blushing. "Maybe so."

"You're not getting any younger, either. Maybe it's time for you to consider settling down and starting a family." Hillary watched the blush deepen on his cheeks. They finished their cigars in relative silence.

"I guess I should freshen up before I go. I'll see you later tonight, Page."

"Aye that you will, Captain. Enjoy your dinner."

"Thank you, Page."

†

Hillary returned to her quarters and washed her face, then brushed her hair before placing a finely wrapped cigar in her breast pocket for Cecil. Darkness was falling over Wright Square, and she shivered as she gazed upon the large oak used for a hanging tree. *I certainly won't miss that grisly sight.*

When she arrived at the DuPont's, Cecelia and her father were sitting out on the front porch, sipping a cool drink of lemonade. "Good evening," she called, as she started up the steps.

"Good evening, Captain," Cecil returned her greeting. "Won't you join us for some lemonade, while the dinner is being prepared?"

"I don't mind if I do, and I brought you a special treat for after dinner." Hillary reached into her pocket to produce the fine cigar. "One of Cuba's finest creations." She watched Cecil's eyes light up, as he accepted her offering.

"That is a special treat. Thank you, Captain."

"My pleasure, sir." She turned to accept the glass of refreshment Cecelia offered, then took a seat beside her.

"We've been blessed with a beautiful evening," Cecelia said. "Our weather tomorrow looks promising as well."

"What time should I meet you?"

"As soon as the livery opens, so we can be on our way."

"Mary has a nice picnic planned for us."

"Who is this Mary?" Cecelia asked.

"I'm almost embarrassed to admit this, but I became a temporary slave owner in Norfolk."

"You did what?" Cecelia cried out in disbelief.

"I was on my way to the general store when I saw this older couple up on the auction blocks. They were house slaves, and their master had passed away. The crowd only wanted to buy field hands, and they weren't interested in an older pair of house slaves. Before I knew it, I had offered five dollars for the couple. Of course, as soon as we left harbor, I gave them back their freedom."

Cecelia was still staring at her.

"I offered to deliver them anywhere they wanted to go, but they've chosen to stay onboard my ship. Mary is a marvelous cook, and Joseph is turning into a fine sailor, under Page's tutelage."

"Well done, good Captain. Did you hear about the slaves that met their death by drowning on their way here?" Cecil asked her with a frown.

"Cecelia told me about them today. That had to be a terrible way to die."

"Indeed, but at least it saved them from a lifetime of slavery," he added.

"That can be said as well."

Cecelia's mother came to the door to call them in for dinner. The aroma of roasted beef, vegetables, and fresh bread, filled the magnificent house. "This is a fantastic meal," Hillary complimented her as they ate.

"I'm glad you approve, Captain." Her mother's tone was rather clipped, and Hillary wondered if she had said something inappropriate. "I understand you spin whimsical tales of life on the sea to my family. Would you care to share one of your recent adventures?"

"Our last trip down in the islands was spectacular. The waters are such a brilliant blue there, and the sands along the beach are as white as pure sugar." All three sets of eyes were on her as she continued. "On an island called Jamaica, they have beautiful beaches, lush tropical rainforests, and mountains. The people are of such diverse character. British, Asian, and African peoples inhabit the island. They have a sauce they use on a variety of meats called 'jerk' which is similar, and yet very different from our barbeque sauces here in America. The rich blend of smoky tastes is enhanced with a zesty ingredient that will have you searching for a mug of something cool to drink."

"That sounds very interesting," Cecil said. "Sometimes the dishes around here could use some extra spice. Not here of course, my dear, this beef is amazing."

"I find it difficult, at times, to leave such a beautiful place. I have purchased a small plantation in the Caribbean and will be retiring there soon," she said without thought. She glanced over and saw Cecelia's face blanch.

"You are very young to be retiring," Cecil said.

"Only from the shipping life, I'll still be raising crops and enjoying the life of a farmer. Page will be taking over the ship, so shipments will be continuing as normal. Don't fret over that."

"That's a relief," Cecil said. "With the boom in the slave trade, it's difficult to find ships that will transport regular cargo."

"Yes, I'm afraid that will continue to drive up everyone's costs," Hillary stated. "The increasing pressure from merchants to transport slaves added to my decision to retire. I will not participate in that evil trade."

Cecil nodded. "I regret that we have participated, even though we only provide a temporary housing space. At least they have a roof over their heads for a short time." He sighed. "I wish there was an alternative, but a more proper method escapes me."

"I wish I had an answer as well." Hillary felt the mood around the table growing somber. "Have you ever tasted fresh coconuts, madam?"

"Well, no I haven't. What is it like?"

"The milk inside is quite thinner than cow's milk but much sweeter to taste. Coconut is used in a lot of the foods in the islands. The snow-white meat is hard and crunchy if eaten in solid form, so it is often shredded or grated. Coconut is also a tasty ingredient for desserts and fresh drinks. I will send some to you, by Page, on our next trip, and also a few fresh pineapples."

"I will look forward to that." She smiled. "Speaking of desserts, Cecelia made a pecan pie. Would you care for a slice with a cup of coffee?"

"That sounds utterly divine."

"Cecelia, would you serve the pie while I bring out the coffee?"

"Yes, Mother."

Hillary watched Cecelia move to a small buffet and serve slices of the rich tasting treat. She had been suspiciously quiet during the meal, yet smiled when she offered Hillary a slice of pie. "Thank you, this looks sinfully delicious."

"I hope you like it. It's my favorite to bake." She blushed as their hands brushed together.

When she returned with coffee, Margaret said, "I understand you ladies are going for a ride to Tybee tomorrow."

"Yes, Cecelia has arranged that for us. I've never taken the opportunity to explore the island," Hillary answered.

"It is still sparsely inhabited, but the marshes and beach are filled with beauty." Cecil looked at his daughter. "It has long been a favorite spot of Cecelia's. As a young child, she loved to frolic in the water and chase the gulls down the beach, while I fished for our meal."

Hillary smiled at Cecelia. "That sounds like a great deal of fun, and I'm sure you're filled with cherished memories."

"Indeed, I am."

Margaret chuckled. "I can remember one day when a great Kemp's Ridley sea turtle came on land to lay her eggs. It was so large, Cecelia climbed on its back for a ride."

Cecelia's eyes lit up. "I remember, that's the year we saw the hatchlings struggling to make it to the ocean."

"Yes. You chased the harassing gulls for an hour to keep them from plucking the babies off the sand as they raced to the water." Cecil smiled at his daughter.

"I couldn't stand to see them killing the babies."

"I know honey, but that's nature's way of ensuring only the best survive," he reminded her.

"Well, I was bent on tipping those odds. I remember crying for an hour until they made it safely into the water."

Margaret looked at Hillary. "We literally had to drag her off the beach that day to get home before dark. She kept insisting there might be more babies."

"I see them often in the ocean. They grow to be huge creatures, who are mesmerizing to watch, as they swim along the boat." Hillary placed her fork across the plate. "That was a delicious meal and an incredible dessert. Thank you both for the wonderful evening."

"Would you like to retire to the porch with Father, while we clean the kitchen?"

"You go ahead too, Cecelia, I can handle these few dishes," Margaret told her.

"No, Mother, it won't take us long together. You can stay for a short while can't you Hillary?"

"Yes, I'll wait until you finish. Then I must return to prepare the men for tomorrow."

Cecil used the flame from the oil lamp to light his cigar. "This is delicious," he said after releasing a plume of fragrant smoke. "You can feel free to send any of these my way." He grinned. "Those Cubans have perfected the art of rolling cigars."

"Indeed, they have. I enjoy one every now and then," Hillary confessed.

Cecil looked at her curiously. "I have to ask you something, while it's just us. Are you planning to ask Cecelia to go to the islands with you?"

Hillary was shocked by his question, amazed at his perception of the friendship between them. She chose to answer him honestly. "I plan to extend that offer to her tomorrow, to see if she's interested."

He chuckled. "Oh, I do believe she is. The islands are all she seems to talk about these days, and now I understand why. Will she be able to visit with us if she chooses?"

"Absolutely. Page will still be transporting your cotton and goods. She can return anytime she wishes."

"Her mother may have some discomfort with this, once she learns of it, but I think I can convince her that Cecelia needs to follow her heart and her dreams. She wants to teach the children on that island of yours to read and write."

"That would be very admirable. They are a poor farming community. I don't know how much of an educational opportunity they have available. It may not be only children who want to learn."

"She would be in heaven. She's always wanted to teach."

"I will be leaving day after tomorrow. Will that create a problem?"

"I will speak to her mother tonight. If Cecelia decides to join you, she'll need to pack her trunks, so don't keep her away all day. I can have her goods delivered early the next morning, so you can get underway."

"That would be perfect."

Cecelia joined them on the front porch, and after a brief conversation, Hillary thanked them once more for a beautiful evening and bid her good-night. Cecelia walked down the steps with her and whispered, "I'm so looking forward to tomorrow."

"So am I. I'll meet you at the livery first thing in the morning. Good night my love."

Cecelia pulled her into a hug, and Hillary desperately wanted to kiss her young lover. "Till tomorrow," Cecelia said and smiled before spinning on her heel.

†

Hillary was still in shock but very pleased by Cecil's revelation. She felt like her feet barely touched the cobbles, as she rushed toward the ship. When she reached the riverfront, Page was sitting on the stone retaining wall, smoking his pipe. He looked up and smiled as she approached.

It was unfortunate that she was focused only on Page. She didn't see the two drunken men stumbling toward her. "You," one of the men called out angrily. "You're the wench who stole my slaves," he accused.

Hillary froze and turned to see the men for the first time. She recognized her accuser as Morgan, the overseer who she had seen before, and another drunken sailor she supposed was part of his crew. "What did you say?" she growled angrily.

"I said, you, stupid wench. You stole my slaves."

"I have never stolen anything, you drunken bastard."

"I know you did. I could see you at the helm as your ship pulled along ours during the storm. You stole what rightfully belonged to me."

"You must be mistaken."

"Make no mistake, I saw you as we rowed to shore."

"Leaving women and children to drown, you cowardly bastard," Hillary spewed her venom toward the filthy man.

"I'll get you for this." He drew his pistol.

Page lunged but was too late to prevent the shot.

Joseph rushed from the deck but could only watch the horror, as his captain crumpled to the ground.

Page flew in a rage, and a fist to the jaw left the man unconscious on the cobblestones. Page grabbed the pistol and told the sailor to take Morgan and leave. He had not seen Hillary collapse to the ground nor the pool of blood growing beside her.

Hillary had seen the gun in the man's hand and prayed that, in his drunken state, he would be unable to fire. Her prayer fell on deaf ears. She heard the shot and turned sideways to reduce the size of the target she made. She felt the searing skin on the left side of her face, and the concussion of the blow made her crumple to the ground in blackness.

The sound of the gunshot brought several more of her crew running to her aid. Manu raced after the two men stumbling away. He beat them near senseless before he could be pulled away.

Joseph and Page arrived at Hillary's side at the same time. Page stepped in the pool of blood and his panic showed on his face. "Joseph, she's been shot in the face," he cried out.

Mary rushed to them and used the hem of her apron to gently dab the blood away from the wound. "We must get her into her quarters, so I can tend to her."

Manu returned, his hands a bloody mess, and helped Page lift Hillary carefully from the ground and carry her onboard. Joseph ran ahead of them and opened the door to her cabin.

"Fetch me some clean water, Joseph," Mary called. "Place her on the bed," she instructed the men.

"What can we do? The doctor in town died of yellow fever last spring," Page said.

Mary saw the wild look of fear in his eyes. "I will do what I can to tend to her. Do we have whiskey onboard?"

"Yes. Manu, run to my quarters. There's a bottle on my cupboard." Page stood beside the bed. "She's not dead, is she?"

"No, she's still breathing, and her heartbeat is strong. The shock left her senseless, and she probably hit her head on the cobbles when she fell."

Joseph arrived with clean water, and Manu returned with the bottle of whiskey. Mary looked up at Joseph after she cleaned the wound on Hillary's left cheek. "I'm going to need my sewing supplies." She looked at the men crowded into the room. "You all need to leave so I can do my work here." She saw Manu's bloody hands. "Are you hurt?"

"Just scrapes and bruises," he said.

"Everyone back on deck," Page instructed. "I'm staying, in case you need help."

Mary nodded. "Fine then, but I hope you can stand watching me sew her skin back together. I can't help you if you faint."

"I'll be fine Mary. Just do what you can for the captain."

She gently turned Hillary's head. As feared, Hillary had struck her head on the cobbles, opening up a small cut. Mary looked up at Page. "Can you sit and place her head in your lap? I need you to hold this against the cut on her head to stop the bleeding, while I tend to her face."

"I can do that." Page sat on the bed and carefully lifted Hillary's head into his lap. Mary handed him a folded piece of sailcloth that he pressed against Hillary's head.

Mary poured the whiskey on another piece of sailcloth and began cleaning around the gunshot. She sighed with relief when she saw that the flesh of Hillary's cheek had split open, but the ball had not penetrated her face. It must have hit a bone and glanced off. She poured a small amount of whiskey directly onto the cheek to flush the wound, and carefully plucked a small fragment of bone from the wound. Hillary didn't make a sound. Mary looked up at Page, who was ghastly white. "You hang in there boy, don't faint on me," she warned gruffly. She handed him the bottle. "Take a drink."

He took a short drink and handed the bottle back to her. "I'm fine," Page said and tore his eyes away from Hillary's face.

"The ball has probably broken her cheekbone, but there is nothing to be done for that. It will have to heal on its own. I can clean and stitch this wound, but that's all I can do. Has that cut stopped bleeding?"

She watched as Page lifted the cloth to see a small amount of blood.

"It seems to have stopped."

"Good, we can wrap a bandage around her head when I'm done, to keep it from breaking open again." Mary continued washing Hillary's cheek with the whiskey, to sterilize the wounded area. "Joseph, thread a needle with that black, heavy thread and dip the needle into the whiskey."

Joseph snapped to work and prepared the needle, tying a knot at the end of the thread before handing it to his wife.

Mary took the needle and looked at Page. "You might want to look away," she warned, as she began closing the wound. "Joseph, please use my scissors to cut a long length of that sailcloth that we can use for a head wrap once I'm done here."

Joseph sat on the end of the bed and cut the cloth she requested. "Will this do?" he asked, holding up the length of cloth.

"That will do well."

"Will she wake soon?" Page asked.

"It's hard to tell," Mary answered. "Her body has taken a terrible shock and has to begin healing itself."

"She's not going to die, is she?"

"No, I don't think so, but she may not wake until tomorrow. She'll be scarred, and her skin will be bruised for a long time, but I think she'll heal. It will be painful for her for a time, as well."

"Should we plan to stay in port for a few more days?"

"There's a doctor in Norfolk. We should stay put until she wakes, but I will feel better if a doctor looks at her soon."

"We could stop in Charleston. It's only a half day away. Surely, they will have a doctor." Page looked anxious and turned away.

"Yes, Charleston would be good. The sooner the better," Mary agreed and continued stitching.

†

When she had done everything she could to close the wound, Mary looked up at Page. "We need to wrap her head. Can you hold that cloth in place?"

"Yes, no problem."

Mary wound the cloth around Hillary's head, across her left eye and cheek. "Joseph, please remove her boots. Let's get her under covers and, hopefully, as comfortable as we can."

With Hillary carefully tucked in, Mary washed her hands. "Will you put on some coffee, Joseph, and will you let the crew know she's going to be fine, Mr. Page?" She dried her hands. "I'll sit with her tonight. You and the others need to get some rest. You have a busy day tomorrow getting the cotton loaded."

Joseph looked at Mary. "I'll stay with you, my love," he told her. "And I promise I'll wake you, Mr. Page, if anything changes."

Page nodded. "I'll check back in with you before I retire."

"Fair enough. Now go." Mary shooed them from the room and took up a seat beside Hillary's bed to start her vigil.

†

Hillary rested during the night. As the sun crested, she began moaning in her sleep. Joseph rushed to her side with worry. "It's good," Mary told him. "Her body is starting to return."

Joseph slumped back in his chair, as Page entered the cabin. "How is she?"

"She rested well and is beginning to come around." Mary smiled up at him.

"I'll sit with her if you'll make breakfast for the crew," he offered.

"I'll send Joseph to spell you when the food is ready, and he can bring you some coffee," Mary said, as he took the seat she vacated. She placed a hand on his shoulder. "The captain is a strong woman, and she'll pull through just fine."

"I hope so, Mary." There were tears shining in his eyes.

†

When Cecelia arrived at the livery, there was no sign of Hillary. She inquired if the owner had seen her, but the man informed Cecelia that she was the first customer of the day. She waited for what seemed an eternity, before deciding to walk to the riverfront to find Hillary. Confused by Hillary's absence, she walked briskly to where the ship was moored.

Several men were working on deck. "Hello, I'm looking for Captain Blythe," she called out.

One of the crew called back to her. "Just a moment Miss." She watched him disappear from the deck.

Page was finishing his meal, when Manu rushed into the galley. "Miss Cecelia is here asking to come aboard."

"Damn, I forgot about their trip today." Page flew from the galley. He rushed down the plank to meet Cecelia and led her over to the retaining wall and sat with her.

Cecelia looked up at him with a puzzled expression. "Page, where is Hillary?"

"There was an accident last night. The captain was wounded, but she will be fine."

Cecelia gasped and clutched at her chest. "What happened?"

"The captain was shot by a drunken man."

"Oh dear." Cecelia fainted.

Page caught her before she fell. "Manu, bring me a wet cloth," he shouted.

Page bathed her face with the cool cloth, until her eyes began to flutter open. She stared up at him with fear.

"I'm sorry, but there was no easy way to tell you. The captain is resting, and Mary assures us she will be fine." He watched her reaction to make sure she wasn't about to faint again. "The shot ripped open her left cheek, and when she fell, she hit her head on the cobbles, knocking her out."

"Can I see her?"

"Are you well enough to walk?" He smiled, as he offered her his hand.

"Yes, I think so." She took his hand, and Page led her onboard the ship.

"She is bandaged, but the bruising covers a large part of her face, due to the trauma she suffered. Don't despair. She will heal fully, in time." Page opened the cabin to Hillary's door, and Cecelia gasped. He held on to her tightly, to ensure she didn't fall if she fainted.

Mary jumped up from her seat. "Put her here." She pointed to her own chair. "I'll get her some coffee."

Cecelia slumped into the chair and took Hillary's hand in hers. "Can she hear me?"

"I don't think so. She seems to be sleeping deeply right now."

"What happened?"

Page shifted nervously, remembering Hillary's warning of secrecy. "Morgan, the overseer of the slaves who went down in the ship, accused Hillary of stealing his goods. He ended the argument by shooting her."

"The slaves? I thought they drowned." Cecelia was even more confused.

"They would have if we hadn't rescued them. The ship was sinking when we pulled up along the wreck. Morgan and his crew had already escaped in a rowboat, leaving the women and children to drown. A few minutes longer and we would have been too late."

"That bastard. How awful."

"We rescued all, but two of the children who had already drowned in the water rushing into the cargo hold."

"What happened to them?"

"We took them where they would be safe from enslavement. We rescued them. We did not steal anything. They were abandoned to die a horrible death, and would have if we hadn't seen the sinking ship." His face wrinkled with worry. "You can never repeat what I just told you or we could all hang."

"I understand. What happened to Morgan? Was he arrested?"

"He and his mate received a good beating from Manu, then fled from the area. If they are smart, they will have left town last night."

"Oh, dear Hillary," Cecelia cried, as she softly stroked Hillary's hand.

†

Hillary heard garbled voices and felt a soft hand stroking her own. She fought to open her eyes, but found she couldn't open her left. She remembered the gunshot and panicked. She feared she had lost an eye. Her throat was on fire and parched. She moved her lips, trying to whet them with her tongue. Her right eye opened, and she found Page and Cecelia beside her bed. She watched Cecelia turn to her, seeming to sense movement. "I'm sorry about our picnic," Hillary croaked out with a raspy voice.

"Oh, Hillary, I don't care about a damned picnic. I'm just happy you're awake."

"I'm awake, but I don't know for how long. I'm tired," she answered. "Page could I get something to drink?"

"I'll be right back."

Mary rushed in. "There you are, Captain. Welcome back." She sat on the edge of the bed.

"What's wrong with me? Why can't I open my left eye?" Hillary fought her rising panic.

Mary smiled. "There's nothing wrong with your eye. I have your head wrapped to protect your injuries. Do you remember being shot?"

"Vaguely." Her answer was a scant whisper.

Page returned with a mug of water. "Here, small sips."

Hillary took the mug and brought it to her lips. "That's much better. Thank you."

"The ball from the pistol ripped open your left cheek and may have broken or chipped a bone. I took out a small piece of bone before I sewed you up. You've got a small cut on the back of your head from hitting the cobbles when you fell, but Page was able to stop the bleeding."

"Thank you for taking care of me."

Hillary looked at Page. "What happened to Morgan?"

"Manu gave them both a pretty good beating and told them to get out of town. They were last seen stumbling toward the bridge," Page said.

"Good for Manu. Is he all right?"

"Some scraped and bruised knuckles, but he's good."

Mary asked, "Could you eat some oats or eggs if I cooked them for you?"

"Maybe later, Mary. Thank you. I just want to sleep right now. Could I have just a few minutes alone with Cecelia? Then I'm going back to sleep."

"Sure." Page and Mary left the room.

"I was going to ask you something special today, before all this occurred."

"What is it?"

"Will you move to the island with me? I was hoping we could leave tomorrow, drop off the cotton, and pick up some tobacco to deliver on our way. Your father said he would have some men bring your trunks down in the morning to load onboard, if you're interested."

Cecelia squealed with excitement. "Of course, I'm interested." Her face scrunched up. "Will you be able to travel by tomorrow?"

"Yes, Page is more than capable of getting us underway. I think I heard something about stopping off in Charleston to see a doctor, but I may have been dreaming."

"I think that would be wise, to have you checked by a doctor."

"I'm going to be sleeping most of the day, so why don't you go get your packing done?"

"I don't want to leave you alone."

Hillary laughed and grimaced. "Oh, don't make me laugh. I promise you, I won't be alone. Go get ready for a new adventure. Just don't bring everything in the house," she teased.

"I promise I won't. Is this what you and Father were talking about last night?"

"Yes, he told me you wanted to teach the children how to read and write. He gave his blessing. You'll have opportunities to return here if you'd like. Page will still be running the shipments."

"This will be so perfect. I'll be back later to check on you." She stood and looked at Hillary. "Would it be all right for me to kiss you?"

"There's nothing wrong with my lips," Hillary said.

Cecelia leaned down and kissed her softly on the lips. "I'll be back later then. I love you, Hillary."

"I love you too, Cecelia. Hurry back to me," she said.

"I will."

She watched Cecelia leave and then closed her eye to drift back to sleep. Her head was beginning to pound. She heard the door open when Mary returned.

"Do you want a shot of whiskey to help your pain?"

"That would be good. My head's about to explode."

Mary poured a shot and handed it to her. She smiled, as Hillary downed the caramel-colored liquid and winced at the taste. "Rest now," she said, as she took the glass from Hillary.

✝

Page was sitting on the retaining wall enjoying his pipe. The men had finished loading the bales of cotton, and the ship rode low in the water. It would, by far, be one of their biggest deliveries of the season. His relaxation was interrupted when the town constable arrived.

"Are you the captain of this ship?"

Page noticed the badge he wore on his coat. "No sir, I'm Page, Captain Blythe's first mate."

"I need to speak to your captain then."

"The captain is currently in quarters recuperating from an injury."

"What kind of injury?"

"A gunshot wound. May I help with something?"

"A gun shot? Why wasn't that reported?"

"I don't believe the captain wishes to press any charges and wasn't in any shape to make a report last night. We were hoping the offender took our advice and left town."

"If it was an ornery cuss by the name of Morgan, you aren't so lucky. He and one of his crew came to my office this morning, looking badly beaten. They spun a tale accusing your good captain of stealing his property. I'd really like to talk to your captain to get his side of the story."

"Her side. Captain Blythe is a woman, Hillary Blythe." Page smiled as he corrected the constable and watched the confusion on his face. "Did Morgan also explain to you what property was supposedly stolen?"

"The scoundrel said your crew boarded his ship and stole some twenty slaves he was bringing into port."

"I don't suppose he mentioned that he and the other two men onboard abandoned ship when they wrecked, or that they left twenty bound and shackled women and children to drown when their miserable excuse for a ship sank?"

"Well no, as a matter of fact he didn't. He led me to believe that they were taken illegally. I did hear about a shipwreck, but didn't make the connection with Morgan. He's a devious bastard, and should have gone down with the ship. The world would be a much better place without his ilk."

"I won't argue with you there, sir."

"What of their physical condition? I'm pretty sure your captain couldn't have done that with a gunshot injury."

"I struck the man, knocking him to the ground, and took away his weapon. One of our crew sent them along their way. They were quite potted and could have put up a fight, but I was so busy tending to my captain, I hardly noticed."

"So, was Morgan the one who shot your captain?"

"Yes, she was ambushed on her way back from dinner at the DuPont's last night. I was too late to reach him before he fired, and she took a shot to her face. It happened right there." He pointed to a section of the street. "You can probably still see the bloodstains."

The constable shook his head. "Amazing he could make that shot."

"That's what I thought too, but when I disarmed him, Captain Blythe had collapsed onto the cobbles."

"Too bad this town no longer has a doctor. He died last spring, during a yellow fever outbreak. Did you tend to her?"

"No, sir, she'd be in much worse shape if I had to doctor her." Page grinned. "One of our other crew was able to tend to her injuries. She was fortunate to be able to turn slightly and the ball split her left cheek, after bouncing off and breaking her cheekbone. She hit her head on the cobbles when she went down, but she was awake earlier today."

The constable looked directly into Page's eyes. "So, do you deny taking the slaves?"

Page decided that honesty was the best way to answer his questions. "No, sir, not at all. We rescued people from drowning on an abandoned ship."

"What did you do with them?"

"Two of the children had already drowned when Morgan forfeited his cargo and his ship. We were on our way to the islands with a shipment of tobacco, and we dropped them at a Methodist mission in Antigua. The missionary woman assured us she could care for them and help them begin new lives." Page made his report, anxious to see what the constable would say.

"So, they were rescued, not stolen?" he asked with a smile growing on his face.

"Yes, sir, and we were behind schedule on our delivery. When we came upon the mission, it seemed like the proper thing to do." *Okay, that wasn't entirely the truth, but it could have been.*

"Are you sure the captain, doesn't care to press charges for attempted murder?"

"She hasn't commented for or against it. I reckon you could ask her for yourself, if you still wish to talk to her."

"I probably should speak with her to be able to close this investigation properly. Would you mind taking me to her?"

"No, sir, follow me." Page tapped out his pipe and led the constable onto the ship. He made eye contact with Manu and nodded for him to move out of sight. His bruised and scraped knuckles would be telling. Page knocked on the captain's quarters, and Mary answered.

Hillary was propped up on the bed. Her face was still horribly bruised and swollen.

"Pardon me captain, but the constable needs to ask you a few questions about last night and our rescue of the slaves," Page said, as the constable followed him inside.

"No, you've pretty much answered all my questions about that. As far as I'm concerned, you rescued drowning victims. Morgan's claim to the slaves and his other cargo were forfeited when he abandoned ship to save his sorry ass. Sorry for my language ma'am."

"No apology needed." Hillary tried to smile and winced at the pain.

"Mr. Page wasn't sure if you wish to press charges of attempted murder against that wretched Morgan," he said.

"As tempting as that sounds, I don't think so. He was a drunken fool that made a poor decision. He's lost his ship and has no means right now. That's justice enough for me."

The constable nodded. "A part of me almost wishes you would, but I hate the sight of hangings."

"Hopefully, it will be a significant amount of time before he can bargain for a new ship," Hillary said.

"I do believe I will send him on his way and threaten him with criminal charges if he returns anytime soon. Once he has a new ship, I won't be able to prevent him from delivering his cargo, but I can ban him from leaving the riverfront."

"That sounds delightful to me."

"I hope you mend well, Captain. Between us, I think highly of what you did for those people. They deserve better.

It's an unfortunate way of life here." He tipped his hat to her. "Have a good day ma'am."

"Thank you, Constable."

Page led him out the door and off the ship, then returned to Hillary's cabin.

"I don't know what you told him, but thank you."

Page smiled at her. "I told him nothing but the truth."

✝

Cecelia rushed back to her home and burst into the house to see her mother in tears on the sofa. "Mother, what's wrong?"

Margaret wiped at her eyes with a handkerchief. "Your Father told me about the captain's offer to take you to the islands with her. I know you won't be able to resist such an offer. The smile on your face when you came in only confirms that."

"It's a great adventure and a huge opportunity for me, Mother. I can do something I've always dreamed of, without risking life and limb. There is no way that, here in Savannah, I would ever be allowed to teach the slave children how to read and write. The plantation owners want them to remain compliant and uneducated."

Margaret nodded. "They don't need to be able to read and write to pick cotton."

"That's exactly what I'm talking about. The color of their skin is the only difference to us. They are still human beings and deserve every chance to better themselves. Not to be physically abused and tortured for not working as quickly as the overseer thinks they should. Do you know what happens to the young girls, Mother? No child should have to endure that."

Margaret sniffled. "I've heard the stories, and I agree."

"I'm afraid that if I stay here, my intolerance of slavery will bring shame to this family, and I would never wish that. I simply can't condone something that is so morally wrong."

"I am proud of you for that, but I don't cherish the thought of my only child being so far away, in some place you've never seen. I know you've been seduced by the stories Captain Blythe feeds you, but it's not the genteel society of Savannah."

"Savannah is losing that reputation by allowing slaves to be delivered and sold in her confines. I won't be gone forever. I can return with Mr. Page, or if you were so inclined, you and Father could come for a visit." She smiled, hopeful that her arguments were successful in relieving her mother's distress.

"Your father did mention that would be possible. He's giving you his blessing."

"I'd like yours as well, Mother. I promise you, if I'm not happy, I will take the first ship home."

"I so want to be selfish, but I cannot deny you the chance to follow your dreams."

Cecelia flew into her mother's arms. "Thank you, Mother. Will you help me decide what to take and assist me in packing?"

†

When Cecil arrived home, he found his wife and daughter packing the last trunk. "Why didn't you come tell me about Captain Blythe getting shot?"

"Shot? Oh my, Cecelia, you didn't tell me either."

"Captain Blythe will be fine. That horrible overseer, Morgan, ambushed her last night when she left here. He accused her of stealing his slaves. In his inebriation, shot her. I saw her this morning, though, and she assures me she will fully heal."

"Page dropped by to see me before I left the office. He said the constable investigated and cleared them of all wrongdoing. I was pleased to hear they had rescued those unfortunate souls from drowning."

"They rescued the slaves from the sinking ship? How brave." Margaret smiled.

"He judged that when Morgan and his men abandoned the ship, their cargo, including the slaves, was forfeit. Hillary and her crew rescued the captives and took them to safety."

"She's really going to be all right?"

"Yes, Mother, we're leaving tomorrow morning and stopping in Charleston. Hillary can be examined by a doctor there. She was very fortunate to not take the full force of the gunshot."

"That's just another example of how the trading of slaves is degrading our beautiful city." Cecil shook his head in disgust. "How is your packing coming?"

"Almost done, Father. I want to go down and visit with Hillary before dinner, if that's all right with you."

"Yes, go ahead. Just be home in time for dinner." He smiled at the excitement he saw in his daughter's eyes. "I've arranged for a couple of men to arrive at day break. They will deliver your trunks to the ship. I just hope a couple will be enough."

"Thank you, Father."

"I'm going to have a drink out on the porch. Will you join me, Margaret, when you two have finished?"

"We'll be down in just a few minutes."

Margaret waited until he left. "You're one hundred percent sure this is what you want?"

"Yes, Mother, I am."

"Go visit with Hillary. We can finish packing this little bit after dinner. I think I need to have a drink with your father."

Hillary chuckled and kissed her mother's cheek. She reached for her hand and walked out to the front porch with her.

"See if that good captain can spare another of those cigars," her father called after her.

"I will, Father," she said, as she rushed toward the riverfront.

CHAPTER FOUR

Two weeks later, they arrived at their new home. Cecelia was in awe of Saint Lucia's beauty. "I had no idea there would be mountains here."

"This is an ancient volcanic island, and the volcano left behind lush fertile soil when it died. The jungles and fields here are perfect for the crops we will raise. Once we get settled, I promise we will explore the island together."

She smiled at Hillary. "I would like that very much. This is so very different from Savannah."

"Yes, it is." Hillary returned Cecelia's smile. It was still painful, but she would do anything for her love. Hillary had healed well, and Mary had removed the stitches from her cheek. The doctor said she'd remain swollen for a while, and the vision in her left eye might be blurry, but he expected her to make a full recovery. He did give her a black patch to wear over her eye for five weeks, until the swelling subsided and her cheekbone healed.

Hillary took a good deal of teasing about her black-patched pirate eye. By the time they had left Norfolk, she was well enough to take short shifts at the helm. Page kept a close eye on her. Cecelia had helped Mary in the galley and learned to cook a few new dishes.

Several of their neighbors stopped by to officially welcome them to Saint Lucia, finding it interesting that a woman now owned the plantation. They were extremely excited about Cecelia's plan to open a small school to teach the island children some basic skills.

Juan was excited to receive the tobacco slips to plant and the coffee seeds that he would start and transplant once the seedlings began to grow. It would take time to grow productive plants, but the weather and Juan's patience were a perfect combination.

Page and the crew had remained for several days. They enjoyed wading through the shallow waters of the cove, trouser legs rolled up to their knees, spearing fish. Manu tried teaching Hillary how to use a cast net, to no avail. "I'd better stick with a spear," she relented.

Now, standing at the end of the dock, they waved as Page and the crew headed back to America to make a delivery. Cecelia gazed at Hillary, who watched the ship sail from sight. "Are you going to miss traveling on the sea?"

"Probably, for a while, but waking up next to you every morning will make it so much easier." Hillary took Cecelia's hand, and they walked back to their small villa. They heard Joseph singing from the back of the house and found he and Mary cultivating the small plot they had chosen for their garden. "Do you want some help?" she called out to them.

"No, Captain, we've got this. You still need to rest." His happiness was evident on his face.

"You can keep me company while I set up my classroom," Cecelia said, as she led Hillary into the villa.

†

A few months after they had settled into their new home, Michael, one of the island children interrupted their leisurely breakfast. "There's a big ship entering the harbor," he cried out, his eyes full of excitement.

"You aren't expecting Page are you?" Cecelia asked.

"Not for another week or so. Let's go see who this is." She took Cecelia's hand in hers, and they walked to the harbor. Michael raced ahead of them to the dock. Hillary was surprised to see her ship dropping anchor in the deeper water. "I wonder what this is about."

"I think we're about to find out." Cecelia pointed to a small rowboat being lowered.

Hillary recognized Manu and Page. "This can't be good news." They rushed to the end of the pier. As they approached, she could see the frown on Page's face.

"Good day, Captain."

"Welcome, Page. I wasn't expecting you so soon."

"There's trouble afoot at the mission," he said, as Manu tossed her a mooring rope.

"What kind of trouble?"

"That damned overseer, Mitchell. You remember the man you threatened when he offered to buy the Africans from you? He has convinced the marshal that Cissy, and Kia,

93

one of the women we rescued, are runaways. He had them arrested and jailed. He was incensed when Elizabeth sold her land to Abraham, and vowed to get revenge on her. Unfortunately, Kia and Cissy have taken the blunt of his revenge. Elizabeth provided papers to prove Cissy's freedom, so she was released, but Kia remains imprisoned."

"When did this happen?"

"Yesterday, we sailed all night to reach you when we got word. Can you think of anything to help them?"

Hillary grinned. "Mitchell and his worthless employer, Mr. Clarke, are terrified of me." She turned back to Cecelia. "Will you please retrieve my pistol? I have business to attend to at the mission."

Cecelia returned carrying the pistol and handed it to Hillary. "You don't plan to use this, do you?"

"Only if it becomes necessary. I'll be back as quickly as possible." She took Cecelia in an embrace and whispered. "I love you and will be back in your arms soon." She turned to the men. "Let's make haste and pray we aren't too late."

†

When they reached the island the next afternoon, Hillary strode angrily down the boardwalk. She could hear the rapid-fire voice of the auctioneer, and knew she might be too late. She spied Mitchell, who had witnessed her approach and was waddling back to the town square for protection. She caught up with him quickly and grabbed him by the back of his foul smelling shirt. She marched him toward his employer, Mr. Clarke, who was loudly protesting Elizabeth outbidding him for Kia. Clarke's eyes grew wide with horror when he recognized Hillary. She pushed Mitchell toward him, with her free hand on the butt of her pistol.

"I am quite surprised, Mr. Mitchell. You failed to heed my warnings." Her steely gaze turned to Clarke. "You need to control your overseer. I believe I made myself clear when I brought the Africans to this island. Mr. Mitchell knew they were not runaways."

"I am most displeased by the way my overseer has handled the situation. I assure you, Captain Blythe, he will be dealt with. I wish no trouble from you. Please accept my deepest apologies for this most unfortunate incident." He bowed and took a step back from Hillary.

"I do hope you are a man of your word. I will be very displeased to have to return to settle matters that should have never transpired. I will take that as a personal affront to my honor, should you fail to control your overseer again." Her fingers gripped the handle of the pistol. "In my world, Mr. Clarke, the only way to handle a dispute of honor is with a pistol. I can assure you that neither you nor Mr. Mitchell possess as keen an eye as I do, with or without my patch. I only need one eye to shoot."

"You have my word, Captain Blythe. I do not wish to enter into a duel with you over a trivial matter such as this."

Hillary released her gaze on him, and then winked at Elizabeth and Kia. "How much did it cost you to win her freedom?"

"Fifty pounds," Elizabeth answered.

"I think it only fair that you reimburse Miss Allen for her troubles."

Clarke growled, but pulled out his purse and handed Elizabeth the money. "This will come out of your wages," he snarled to Mitchell, who wisely remained silent.

Page and Manu had secured the ship and caught up with them, as Clarke and Mitchell turned to leave. Page looked at Hillary. "Is everything in good repair, Captain, or should we take these men to task?"

Clarke looked horrified and nearly ran over Mitchell to get away from the small group that had gathered.

"No, Page, I think we're in good shape here."

Hillary, Page, and the crew spent the evening at the mission to ensure everything was, indeed, in good shape. Mr. Barlow came by with papers to make Kia a free person, and the next morning, after a hearty meal, they set sail for home.

✝

The island children filled Cecelia's small school, eager to learn. Hillary walked by one afternoon, and Mary was sitting in a small circle of children as they practiced writing the alphabet. Mary would bring the children an afternoon snack and join them in their lessons. Joseph had shared with Hillary how proud Mary was to be able to write her own name and prepare a list of goods to purchase. Tears shone in his eyes as he spoke. Joseph was just as proud.

Hillary enjoyed spending time with the children when she could, spinning wild tales of life on the ocean. Even after her wound had healed, she found it necessary to wear the eye patch outside. The sun's glare gave her headaches if she didn't wear the protective covering. She frequently wore her patch when she spoke with the children, to give them the feel of the daring pirates she often spoke of in her stories. Sharing with the island children reminded her of the children of the missionary school, and she wondered how life was going for the women and children she and her crew had rescued.

Page and the crew continued to stop by the mission. They brought back reports of a prosperous ending for the rescued women and children. Hillary often dreamed of going back to the island to visit, but life on the plantation occupied most of her time and energy.

✝

One evening, Hillary sat out on the dock enjoying a cigar, as the sun drifted beyond the horizon. Cecelia's head rested on her shoulder. "Did you hear it?" Hillary asked.

"Hear what, my love?"

"The sizzle as the sun sank down into the water." She chuckled.

"No, but it was a beautiful sunset. Thank you for bringing me here."

"It feels like home now that you're here with me. Mary and Joseph have settled in well, too." Hillary sighed, as Cecelia laid her head back on her shoulder. "I think I'll rig up some fishing lines tomorrow."

"You just can't stay idle, can you?"

"It's not in my nature. I think fishing, and maybe some crab traps, would give us seafood to enjoy until the animals are big enough to slaughter."

"I know we need fresh meat, but those animals are so adorable."

"Don't go getting attached to them, my love. They will provide food to keep us healthy." Hillary feared her warning was already too late. Maybe she should move the animals to the far side of the property, to keep them from being pets for Cecelia. "Speaking of food, why don't we go see what feast Mary has prepared for us tonight?"

"I'm actually feeling hungry," Cecelia said.

†

Hillary closed the door to their bedroom and began to slowly undress Cecelia. Her lips caressed the exposed skin, as her hands slipped the garments from her body. "I could never tire from the taste of you," she said, as she kissed down Cecelia's neck. She cupped Cecelia's breast, as she bent down to place gentle kisses on the milky flesh.

"You make me shiver with anticipation," Cecelia whispered, as she ran her fingers through Hillary's hair. "I need to feel your skin on mine." She moaned, as Hillary's teeth grazed across her nipple.

"Climb onto the bed. I'll undress and join you." Hillary stood and kicked out of her boots, as she pulled her shirt over her head. She locked eyes with Cecelia, who stretched out on the bed. Passion pooled in Cecelia's dark eyes, revealing her hunger. Hillary smiled, as she climbed onto the bed. She lowered her body gently onto Cecelia, and felt Cecelia's hands stroke down her back, pulling her hips deeply into Cecelia's body.

"That feels so much better."

"I agree." Hillary breathed across her skin, as she began undulating her hips. She smiled at Cecelia and then captured her lips in a fevered kiss.

They made passionate love, deep into the night. When Cecelia was finally nestled in her arms, Hillary brushed a strand of hair away from her face. "I'm so glad I met and fell in love with the DuPont chandler's daughter."

"And she's delighted to be loved by a handsome captain."

†

Cecelia traveled back to Savannah twice more, the final time to learn that her parents had died in a yellow fever outbreak, only weeks before her return. Her uncle had taken care of the arrangements and settled the estate, including a large sum of money left on her behalf. She visited the cemetery, placing fresh flowers on the graves. Cecelia arranged for the last of her belongings to be stowed away onboard the ship, thus closing out her life in Savannah. There was no reason for her to return, and she welcomed the thought of living the rest of her days beside Hillary.

Hillary enjoyed sitting on the dock watching the sunset and on occasion longed for the days spent out on the open waters. Then she would hear the sound of Cecelia's laughter, or feel her presence when she joined her for her daily ritual, and she knew she was exactly where fate intended her to be.

BOOK TWO

FORBIDDEN LOVE

ANNETTE MORI

CHAPTER FIVE

Elizabeth Allen sat on the floor with her skirt gathered around her and the book propped in her lap. The children's eager faces turned toward her, riveted to every word. She knew she should be reading from the Bible, but she couldn't help pulling from her treasured stack of books when they begged her to read another adventure. *Gulliver's Travels* by Jonathan Swift was a popular choice.

Teaching the innocent children was something innately suited to her temperament. Children did not see color as they played together or listened to the stories she read to them. The mostly dark faces sat alongside the pale-skinned children; their only care in the world was to listen to Elizabeth spin her tales. Sometimes, she would set aside her books and make up stories for the children.

Beyond the walls of the church and on the large sugar plantations, this peace and tranquility did not exist. There were two Antiguas, in her opinion; the cruel Antigua that continued to perpetuate the mistreatment of human beings by the ownership of slaves, and the world inside the walls of her church. Elizabeth was appalled to learn that not only the British and Loyalists owned slaves. A fair number of former slaves, now free and prosperous, also maintained the abhorrent institution of slavery.

The heavy wooden door banged loudly against the wall. Cissy's generous lips often revealed her gleaming white teeth in a mischievous smile, but today the whites of her wide-open eyes remained prominent in the dim light of the church, as she blew through the door.

Cissy was a former house slave, rescued and now free to work side by side with Elizabeth. She'd been brought over from Georgia and retained the languid southern drawl learned on the cotton plantation. Cissy wasn't known for her discretion and often passed tales along as a favorite form of entertainment. She seemed to hover for a chance to learn the most up to date news from the port. For greater effect, Cissy would embellish to the point of relaying untruths or distortions that often scared the young children and garnered harsh words from Elizabeth. While Elizabeth's stories were full of adventure and romance, Cissy enjoyed spinning tales of a more ominous nature.

"Miss Allen, Miss Allen, Captain Blythe has slaves on her ship." Cissy rushed her words. "I seen 'em with my own two eyes."

"Cissy, don't you dare tell tall tales at the expense of the good captain," Elizabeth admonished.

"I swears I'm not tellin' tales, Miss. This time it's true. Theys young too. All women and children. I seen them frightened white eyeballs peekin' out on the deck. They was tryin' to hide, but I seen 'em."

Elizabeth frowned. Normally, when Cissy was challenged, she would amend her story closer to the truth or back down and admit to telling a tall tale. Cissy was a curious young woman and paid close attention to the comings and goings of the harbor, especially after Captain Blythe had given her the spyglass. She was enamored with the handsome captain and always wanted to hear her stories of harrowing adventures at sea. Cissy would embellish the stories with sea monsters when retelling them to the children.

"Cissy, did you use Captain Blythe's spyglass?"

Cissy nodded. "Yes'm."

Elizabeth had a bad feeling. "Cissy, did you talk to anyone else about this?"

"No, ma'am," she answered.

Elizabeth pierced her with a look of challenge. "No one?"

"Well maybe Mr. Clarke. He was comin' out of the tavern and asked me where I was runnin' to. He mean, so I's got scared and tol' him what I seen."

"You wait here with the children, Cissy, and don't move. Understand?" Elizabeth picked herself up from the ground and gathered her skirts.

"Yes'm." Cissy's eyes were as wide as saucers.

"I'm going to the harbor to see about this. Don't scare the children with any of your tall tales of sea monsters."

"No, ma'am, I won't." Cissy sat on the wood floor and grinned at the children.

Elizabeth wished she had time to be more specific with her directive. She heard Cissy beginning a story of the sugar cane monster. "At night, when it's as dark as my skin…"

She had to get to the ship and find out what Cissy was talking about. Determined to find a place for the women and children in her vast network of ex-slaves, Elizabeth hurried to the port. Each household could surely handle one or two more mouths to feed if it meant none of the ex-slaves would end up on one of the sugar plantations. She would talk to her father about housing another person in their comparatively meager holdings. The large plantations had overtaken nearly all of the smaller parcels of land, but her father managed to retain his assets, working alongside his freed slaves to make ends meet. Too many slaves on the prosperous plantations had died of disease or simply disappeared. The callousness turned her stomach every single time she listened to the scandalous chatter.

†

Elizabeth clip-clopped along the old wooden planks of the harbor on Antigua, grabbing the hem of her long skirt and lifting the many layers. In the heat, she wished she could bypass the formal dress, but her father had not loosened his stance on what was appropriate for a young, unmarried woman hoping to catch the eye of an eligible man. At least the fashion of the day allowed a loose-fitting neckline gathered over her ample breasts with a simple drawstring.

Her father was a good man, driven by his deep faith. As Loyalists, John Allen and others had received land grants from the Crown after the American Revolution. Unlike their

104

neighbors on Antigua, Elizabeth's father did not have the stomach for running a plantation if it meant owning slaves. His ideals aligned more with the new Methodist church.

He would approve of her actions because of the welcoming stance of their church toward everyone, regardless of the color of their skin or their gender. She lamented that his progressive stance did not extend to her preference to never marry. Her work with the church was too important to divert any of her valuable time to a husband and children.

Elizabeth never knew why she rejected the terms used for the beautiful, dark-skinned people. Calling them Negroes or coloreds set them apart in a way that made her uncomfortable. Her father reasoned that descriptions were a necessary evil and perhaps Africans might be acceptable as that was no different than British or Colonial.

Elizabeth knew that talk spread quickly. If Mr. Clarke discovered the female captain was carrying Africans in her hold, he would try to purchase them at a bargain. She was determined to reach the port before George, the overseer of the Clarke plantation, tried to lay claim to the women. Elizabeth didn't believe the handsome and imposing captain would sell the women and children, but she wanted to provide a viable option; her mission would bring the women into their fold and teach them the word of the Lord. She refused to believe that Captain Blythe was now involved in the slave trade.

Breathing a sigh of relief, she hurried past the rotund, red-faced man huffing and puffing his way to the harbor, as Captain Blythe was directing her crew. Catching a whiff of his foul body odor combined with the strong smell of the sea caught her off guard, and she held her breath until she was well past the uncouth man. Elizabeth looked right and left in desperation. She hoped she was not too late. None of the African women and children were in plain sight. George was still working hard to catch his breath as he made his way to the harbor, so she knew they had not been sold to the cruel man.

"Captain Blythe," Elizabeth called out.

The piercing blue eyes turned in her direction and a smile grew on Captain Blythe's face. "Miss Allen, you have saved me from attempting to seek you out. I was about to come see you and your father. I was hoping you may be able to provide assistance with a delicate matter." The tall woman took several purposeful strides to meet Elizabeth.

"I do hope this has to do with the rumors about the African women and children on your ship who require assistance."

The captain's gleaming white teeth flashed at Elizabeth. "Indeed it is, Miss Allen, indeed it is. I knew this was the best option for them. They have been through a harrowing experience." She looked away, and Elizabeth caught the glistening in her eyes. "We were unable to save two of the children. They were all left shackled together as their ship went down. Drowning was inevitable. I could not allow that to happen. My cook, Mary, has helped to settle them, but their English is very limited. She could teach them only a few words on the short journey here."

"I know a few African words, and there is another in our congregation who speaks many of the different African dialects. I believe, between the two of us, we will be able to help them transition to island life."

"Captain Blythe, Captain Blythe." George was breathing heavy, as he hurried to greet the captain. "I will pay you handsomely for the merchandise. You are a businesswoman. Surely you can appreciate receiving fair payment for those goods."

Captain Blythe narrowed her eyes, and Elizabeth heard a raging storm in the captain's measured question. "What merchandise are you speaking of?"

"The Negroes," he answered. "The condition they are currently in is not a problem for us. We will whip them into shape in no time."

"Mr. Mitchell, you have received incorrect information. There is not enough money in the world to entice me to sell one human being to another. I abhor slavery. Surely, you know of my position on the matter."

"But, but," he blustered. "You have Negroes on your ship. Why would you carry that cargo if not to sell them?"

"That is none of your concern. This matter is closed. I will not reconsider my position. Be off with you. I have business with Miss Allen and her father that does not involve you."

"You will regret this, Captain Blythe."

The captain stalked toward George and towered over him as she closed the distance between them. "Are you threatening me, Mr. Mitchell? Because if you are, I believe my honor is at stake. The only reasonable solution would be a duel. I look forward to a duel with you." Her eyes roamed up and down his body. "You'll make for a very large target, easy to hit."

Elizabeth covered her mouth in an attempt to hold back her laughter.

"Don't be ridiculous," George sputtered. "You are a woman."

"A woman who possesses a much sharper eye and skill with a pistol than you. You are a coward, Mr. Mitchell. If you make trouble for Miss Allen or her father after I leave, I will return and ensure that my honor is avenged. Do I make myself clear?"

George spun around and scurried away muttering, "Unnatural woman."

"I'm sorry Captain, Cissy was using the spyglass you gave her and saw them on your ship. That is why George came waddling along so quickly."

The captain smiled. "How is Cissy?"

"Scaring the young children with her horror stories. She hangs on your every word and twists them around to make the stories bigger and more frightening."

"That one has an imagination. Perhaps you should have her write them down. The older children might appreciate the tall fables and not cause you to chastise her so." Grinning, the captain stepped forward and held out several silver pieces. "Please, take these to help with the care of the women and children."

"Thank you for your generosity, Captain."

The captain tipped her hat. "No, thank you, Miss Allen. I am relieved they will have a better life in the care you and your father will provide. I'll have Manu and Joseph ferry them ashore."

†

Elizabeth tried to hold her emotions in for the sake of the frightened women and the small children clinging to them, their thin, frail bodies adorned in rags. She suspected the captured slaves had been in far worse condition prior to

Captain Blythe saving them. That thought nearly broke her heart.

She attempted to calm them with words of assurance, but was grateful when Abraham Gilbert met them on the beach and translated for her. She didn't have the luxury of gathering others at such short notice.

Although Abraham had an imposing presence (he stood well over six feet tall and had broad, heavily muscled shoulders), his voice had a smooth, soft timbre that often lulled the most frightened child. He was a handsome man, with warm, brown eyes and a wide, welcoming smile. Many of the island women had hoped to catch his eye, but none stood a chance against Rebecca. Her beauty, both inside and out, as well as her quiet intelligence and insight, had captured his attention from the first moment he laid eyes on her. After only a short time, they had married and continued to be a stable presence on the ten-acre plantation her father owned. Abraham worked the small parcel of land John Allen encouraged him to tend for his own profit. Elizabeth often saw Abraham gently making suggestions to her father on how to endure the many challenges of harvesting sugar cane.

As she walked along the path to the church, the ugliness of the situation was in such contrast to the beauty of the island. Since Elizabeth had first set foot in her new home, she thought the chain of hills in the distance beautifully romantic. The luxuriant vegetation and tall sugar stalks were liberally sprinkled on those very summits. The assemblage of mountains dotted the landscape as far as her eyes could see, more picturesque than the rolling hills in England.

When they reached the wooden church with its gray weathered boards, Elizabeth turned to Abraham. "Mr. Gilbert, would you please gather as many of our congregation as you can? Any who would be willing to take in one or two of these rescued Africans. And perhaps you could find my father, as well."

"Yes, Miss Allen, I can do that. The missus and I have room for one, maybe two, if there is a little one that needs to stay with their mother," Abraham answered.

"Are you sure? I know your house is small. Isn't Rebecca expecting?"

Abraham's toothy grin widened. "She is. Her belly is large, so it should be any day now. But we have room."

"Bless you, Mr. Gilbert, for your kindness."

"Miss Allen, it is your kindness that shines bright for us all. I'll be back shortly." Abraham quickly exited the church, and Elizabeth turned toward the others.

The group of women and children huddled close together, avoiding Elizabeth's gaze as they looked to the ground. She had almost forgotten about the children in the story circle, until she saw small faces looking curiously in her direction. Cissy was uncharacteristically quiet.

"Oh dear. I'm sorry, children. Today's lessons will need to be shortened. There is a new group of worshipers that we need to help settle. Cissy, you're always quick to add chatter to a room; perhaps you can welcome them."

"Yes'm." Cissy stood and began speaking in low tones, encouraging the eighteen new congregants to come further into the rustic sanctuary. Their simple church might not compare favorably to the beautiful English bricks of St. John's Cathedral perched atop the hill. Before the big fire, St. John's was not much different than her own church, but today, its grand remodel overshadowed all other places of worship.

The newcomers maintained their tight pack and chose to sit on the floor next to the children, rather than scatter throughout the wooden benches. One regal young woman remained standing, curiously observing Elizabeth with round chocolate eyes set above full lips on a face of smooth, ebony skin. The swell of her breasts was barely hidden beneath the rags draped over her thin body.

Had this young woman been sold into slavery, she would have been repeatedly violated by some overseer, or at best, ended up as mistress to one of the plantation owners. The owners fancied themselves gentlemen and would not consider taking liberties with their slaves barbaric or inappropriate. Having an African mistress to satisfy their needs was commonplace. A proper wife could not be expected to serve this purpose.

Elizabeth felt compelled to reassure this young woman and took several steps to close the distance between them, touching her on the arm. The woman tentatively reached up to run her fingers through strands of strawberry-blonde hair that had escaped their pins. Elizabeth held still and closed her eyes to the touch. The woman had likely never seen light hair and eyes. Captain Blythe's hair was always pulled back and hidden under her hat.

Elizabeth pointed to herself. "Elizabeth."

The young woman let her finger slide through the strands of Elizabeth's hair and pointed to herself. "Kia."

Elizabeth nodded. "Kia is a beautiful name. I won't be giving you another."

Looking away to hide an immediate sense of revulsion, Elizabeth realized what she'd just done. The arrogance of the Americans and her own countrymen took away everything from these beautiful people: their pride, their freedom, and their given names. She'd so easily fallen into the trap of treating grown women as children and replacing their beautiful tribal names with Christian ones.

When her gaze returned to the curious brown eyes, Elizabeth felt a strange stirring inside. She knew she needed to make a place for Kia. She could not expect the other free Africans to make room in their small houses for these rescued slaves, unless she was willing to open her own home. *Father will understand.*

CHAPTER SIX

The path to the small, ten-acre sugar plantation Elizabeth and her father tried desperately to maintain, was well-worn. Elizabeth noted, with interest, that this path was far easier to travel than the spacious streets close to the harbor. No one seemed to pay much attention to their care. The unpaved streets were overwrought with prickly pear and scrub brush.

The past year had not been prosperous, and they were barely hanging on. Despite Abraham's wise advice, very little of the sugar cane would survive the severe drought and harsh sun.

Elizabeth's father insisted she remain dedicated to her work with the church and not worry about the troubles with their sugar cane crop. Field work was hot and difficult, and he feared her fair skin would burn, even with a large hat to protect her. Despite her efforts to avoid the punishing sun, unsightly freckles dusted along her nose, face, and exposed arms.

That morning, her father had seemed lethargic, almost as if he'd finally decided to give up and move back to England. Elizabeth feared his commitment to the church and to the people of this poor island was waning. She pushed open the heavy wood door of the stone building. Abraham had informed her that her father had not come into the fields yet. That fact alone was unusual.

"Father, Father, I have news."

Kia stood meekly by her side. Elizabeth had led her home by the arm and now gestured for her to sit. Elizabeth went in search of her father and gasped when she realized he remained in his bed, chills ravaging his body.

"Oh, Father, why didn't you tell me you'd fallen ill?"

He lifted his fevered eyes. "I seem to have caught the fever."

Running from her father's bedroom, her eyes darted around, searching for a cloth to wipe his fevered brow. She spotted Kia and was torn between caring for her father and settling her guest. *The rags on her body must go, and I need to prepare a meal for the half-starved woman.*

Kia must have sensed her despair. She watched Elizabeth carefully, following her to the cistern where she dipped the cloth into the cool water. Elizabeth ran back inside, pressing the piece of cotton against her father's forehead.

So immersed in caring for her father, Elizabeth didn't register Kia's absence until she heard rustling in the main living area. The deep rumbling of Abraham's voice caught her attention, and she gathered her skirts and reluctantly left her father's bedside.

"Miss Allen, Kia has come to get me. She recognized the fever but doesn't know about the native plants to help soothe Mr. Allen. With your permission, I will teach her. We will bring back a tea for him to drink." His eyes revealed his sadness. "It is in God's hands now."

She returned to the sick room and noted his pallid complexion. Elizabeth was not under any illusion her father would recover. Few men of his age and declining health could survive yellow fever. The odds were not in his favor. She gathered his hand in hers and continued to wipe his brow. A response was beyond her capability in her moment of grief.

"We will go now," Abraham announced.

Kia advanced two tentative steps in Elizabeth's direction and touched her head, carefully enunciating, "Kia help Elizabeth." Every syllable was uttered with precision, and it warmed Elizabeth's heart to hear those words.

†

Kia had not seen eyes the color of the sky until her own eyes rested on the captain who had saved her and the others from the ravages of the angry sea. She wondered if only the women of this new land looked at the world through this pale color and if this prevented them from seeing the world with the same vibrancy she observed. She hoped not, for both women had showed her kindness.

Before reaching land, she'd noted the great quantities of gulf weed floating on the clear blue waters. She'd wanted to reach out and scoop them in her hands, so she could see the beauty of the blue hidden by the weed. On the various occasions the captain allowed them on deck, she gazed with wonder on the sea, especially when the moon left a small reflection on top of the water. In one moment such beauty, but in another, the terrifying angry gray skies pummeled the ship with wind and rain. The clouds would hide the moon's light and dash her spirits.

Earlier, she had reached up to touch Elizabeth's golden hair with its shining, reddish highlights. She was pleased when the strands felt as soft to the touch as she thought they would. Elizabeth was pleasing to look at. The women of her village would consider her exotic, and the men would desire her as much as they had vied for Kia's attention. Men like Tou. She refused to join with the prominent first son of the neighboring village, and he led the raid against her tribe. She'd made a grave mistake by dishonoring him and had paid with her freedom.

Blue was a cold color, but Kia saw the warmth Elizabeth conveyed when she gazed in her direction. Kia decided she liked the color blue. Tou's dark-brown eyes had turned as black and impassive as death when the men placed her in shackles and took her away.

The space allotted to her on the ship was little more than five feet by sixteen inches. She had only enough room to lie on one side. The stench on the ship and the rolling waves increased the sickness. Soon, bile and excrement sloshed all around her. As the sloop listed on its side and water came rushing in, she still could not wash away the smell or the memory. Now, the desire to bathe in the sea warred with her fear of death, even as the furious waves calmed to a gentle rolling.

She was no longer afraid, as she followed Elizabeth along the path to the stone dwelling. But she grew frustrated when Elizabeth called out to someone inside. The words were foreign to Kia. Had a man claimed her as his wife? Was Elizabeth calling out to her husband?

When Elizabeth returned to the large open area of the stone hut, her eyes darted everywhere. Kia followed her into the small room off to the side. When familiar-looking blue eyes opened, Kia understood the sickness. The man was not long for this world, but she could seek out the plants that might help. It pained Kia to see how Elizabeth also recognized the inevitability of his death. Kia was desperate to learn the words to communicate with Elizabeth.

✝

"Leave this godforsaken place," her father muttered in his delirium. "I shouldn't have brought you here."

"Shhh, Father. I love this place, these people, whom we are charged with ministering to."

Beads of perspiration covered her father's body, as he moved around in his sweat-soaked sheets. His restlessness was painful to watch. "A naval officer. You must find yourself an honorable officer to marry, who will take you away."

"I will do no such thing."

"I'm sorry Anne, I'm sorry," he cried out.

Elizabeth didn't know how to settle her father. He was calling out, apologizing to his dead wife. He had brought her to the island with him, instead of leaving her with her aunt. That aunt would undoubtedly have assured her marriage to a proper gentleman.

"Shhh, Father, shhh. I promise, I will find love and marry. We'll make this plantation survive and continue the ministry." She didn't know why she made that promise, other than her need to give him some measure of tranquility in his final days on earth.

"Good, good." Her father closed his eyes and seemed to settle.

Pulling the now warm cloth from his forehead, Elizabeth left his bedside to gather fresh water. The tea that Abraham and Kia had made remained only partially consumed on the bedside table.

Elizabeth was surprised to find Kia sitting at the large table with Abraham and his wife, Rebecca. Her belly protruded in front of her but didn't stop her from fussing over the table and the considerable spread of food. Elizabeth didn't realize how many hours had passed since she'd found her father in his weakened condition.

Realizing that Kia would not reach for the salted beef, guinea corn, sweet potatoes, plantains, or bananas until given permission, Elizabeth piled a plate high and set it in front of Kia. The dirty clothing still hung loosely over Kia's body, and Elizabeth mentally chastised herself for not finding appropriate clothing for the young woman. She frowned and decided to tend to Kia before returning to her father's bedside.

"Mr. Gilbert, will you please explain to Kia that I would like to take her back to my bedroom and give her something more…suitable to wear."

Abraham nodded and began speaking in his soothing, low-toned voice, articulating the unfamiliar syllables in the African language. Kia seemed curious, her eyes traveling

118

over Elizabeth's gathered neckline and long flowing skirts, then returning to rest on her own rags.

"Abraham, perhaps you could gather water for me, as well," Elizabeth added.

When Elizabeth first arrived on the island, she was amazed at the ingenious nature of collecting water. The natives were eager to teach her how to accumulate rainwater in large, stone cisterns drawn from the reservoirs and filtered through the native Barbados stone. Fresh springs were scarce on Antigua. She'd taken a chance to sip a small amount of water and found it exceedingly soft, with a more pleasing flavor than any water found in her native England.

As Abraham left to retrieve the water, Elizabeth touched Kia's elbow and led her back to the bedroom they would need to share in the small home. Elizabeth reasoned her large feather bed would have ample room for two.

Pulling a simple, cotton frock from the armoire, Elizabeth set the dress aside on her bed. The garment was light enough to be comfortable, but she hoped it would cover Kia's dark skin enough to hide her womanhood. Elizabeth shook her head, trying to remove the vision of Kia's large breasts and erect nipples, obvious against the sheer fabric. None of the people of the island gave a second thought to revealing clothing and immodesty when bringing in a new crop of slaves. It was as if they were immune to the degradation of simple human compassion this caused. The indelicacy of the slaves' dress was looked upon as nothing more than standard fare. They were not considered to exist on any higher rung than farm animals.

A light knock on her door jarred Elizabeth from her thoughts. She moved her hand down Kia's arm in a gesture

119

of assurance, as she opened the door to Abraham who was carrying the large bucket of fresh water.

"Thank you, Mr. Gilbert."

"Welcome, Miss."

She accepted the heavy bucket and shut the door. She carried the bucket to the dresser and poured the contents into the basin sitting on top. She opened the top drawer of her sturdy, mahogany dresser and pulled a clean handkerchief from inside. Opening another drawer, she removed undergarments and base layers, to assure a certain level of modesty, and set them next to the frock she'd chosen earlier. She dipped the cloth in the fresh water and rubbed it on the soap sitting next to the basin, then squeezed out the excess water. She slowly approached Kia and demonstrated her intent by wiping the cloth over her own arm. She pushed aside the dirty rag Kia wore, until it lay in a pool at her feet. She would burn the item later. Elizabeth did not want Kia reminded of any part of her journey to Antigua.

Kia blinked but remained still, and Elizabeth assumed she had not understood her small demonstration. She gently caressed Kia's glistening, ebony skin, removing the dirt and grime. Elizabeth couldn't help noticing the puckering of Kia's nipples, as she brought the cloth over her breasts and wiped the subtly heaving mounds. A flutter in her stomach left Elizabeth confused, as she continued to bathe Kia. She was surprised when Kia reached up, taking the cloth from her hand and bringing it over her cheek. Kia's shy smile erupted to show even, white teeth in sharp contrast to her beautiful skin that begged to be touched.

Elizabeth took Kia's hand with the cloth and placed both back on Kia's collarbone to have her continue to bathe herself. The indentation below Kia's neck, sitting innocently between the protruding bones, caused a stirring inside Elizabeth. The onslaught of those feelings felt unnatural—at least that was what the church taught. She knew that she was no longer helping to show Kia how to bathe. She was enjoying the feel of Kia's body, as she moved her hand along her soft curves. At least the malnourishment hadn't removed all evidence of her womanhood. Pointing to the frock and the many layers of undergarments required of women, Elizabeth pantomimed pulling the dress over her head.

She nearly ran from the room and the burgeoning feelings she was sure would cause her to burn in hell. She rested her head against the door for a moment, before returning to Rebecca and Abraham, who were looking at her inquisitively.

"Rebecca, I need to check on Father. Will you ensure that Kia is able to put on the frock I've set aside for her?"

"Yes'm."

Elizabeth remained flustered; her interaction with Kia seemed too intimate for a proper British woman. She forgot to gather a new cloth for her father. When she returned to his bedroom, his body lay still in the bed. At first, she believed he was resting peacefully. Upon closer inspection, she realized his chest was not moving. She bowed her head, knowing without touching his skin that he had passed to the other side. Surely, he had joined his wife in heaven. Her heart was so full of sadness; she wasn't sure how she would continue without his steady hand. Slumping on the chair beside his bed, she took his already chilling hand and began to softly cry for the loss of a great man. She wondered if this was her retribution for having unnatural feelings.

She felt a presence behind her. Even though she knew this was exactly why God would continue to punish her, she welcomed the gentle caress on her back, the loving fingers that brushed the fabric of her dress, traveled to her neck, and burrowed into her bun.

The words were repeated again with precision. "Kia help Elizabeth."

†

Rebecca watched with interest how Kia never left Elizabeth's side, nearly anticipating her needs. After observing a task, Kia would quietly take over. She was the one providing the traditional black ribbons for the mourners to tie around their arms.

The coffin sat on the table. Typical to the customs of the island, several women sobbed and wailed over the wooden box with Mr. Allen resting inside. Kia stood to the side, looking curiously at what must have been an odd spectacle to her.

Rebecca had expected the immense turnout and hoped Elizabeth would feel pleased by the respect paid by so many that Mr. Allen had ministered to. Abraham took charge and assembled the mourners in a specific order to begin the procession. Even after several years of friendship, Elizabeth continued to address Abraham as Mr. Gilbert. Rebecca understood this was a gesture of respect, but was glad Elizabeth greeted her with much less formality. The familiarity had taken several years to develop, yet with Kia there was an almost instant intimacy. That fact was not lost on Rebecca's keen assessment.

Rebecca was concerned for Elizabeth and Kia. While the island did not discourage relationships between natives or free Africans, their stance on unnatural actions between men was strictly forbidden and punishable by hanging. The teachings from the church mostly covered the acts by men, but it was understood to include intimacy between women. Rebecca feared for the trajectory of the friendship she saw building between the two women.

"It is time, Elizabeth. Your father will be put to eternal rest." Rebecca slid her arm inside Elizabeth's and led her to join the procession. Kia watched intently and followed by slipping her own arm inside Elizabeth's on the opposite side. The three women walked side by side, slowly following the nearly one hundred mourners. John Allen was a well-loved man.

CHAPTER SEVEN

On the day of the funeral, work on the plantation stopped for several hours. The field hands who had worked alongside John Allen paid their respects. Elizabeth knew very little of the plantation business. She understood the agreements her father had made with several of the freed Africans who worked small patches of the sugar cane fields. His will had passed the entire ten-acre plantation to her along with small provisions for Cissy, Abraham, and his wife, Rebecca.

Elizabeth wasn't worried about her own ability to survive. Provisions were made by her father, prior to his death, through an indenture prepared by the solicitors in the astonishing sum of £20,000. Elizabeth had no idea her father had amassed so much wealth, and she wondered why she didn't know this fact. She vowed to live her life in humility, as her father had. There was no need to adopt any extravagance when all her needs were met. She felt guilty knowing that, while her survival did not depend on the success of the plantation, so many others would not endure without a healthy crop. She felt the weight of that responsibility, as she suspected her father had before his death.

The drought had wreaked havoc on the sugar cane fields and that worried everyone. Elizabeth sat with her head in her hands, wondering what to do next. She didn't realize that Kia had come into the room until she sat in the closest chair and whispered in her precise voice, "Elizabeth."

Elizabeth lifted her head and looked into warm brown eyes that held such a range of emotions she could already read. Today she recognized warmth, concern. Kia smoothed the wrinkles on Elizabeth's forehead with the tips of her fingers. The heavy weight on her shoulders always drew those lines, as she considered those who depended on her for their very survival. She couldn't sell the plantation to Mr. Clarke. That would surely mean the demise of those families who worked the parcels of land her father could not handle all on his own.

"Oh, Kia, what am I to do without Father? I know nothing of plantation business. I am a teacher, not a plantation owner."

"Teach Kia. Abraham help," Kia offered.

Kia was picking up English quickly, but the words she used could mean so many things. Kia was bright and insightful, that was evident over the last few days. Without thinking, Elizabeth grasped Kia's hand and held it briefly. The touch settled her, as she began to evaluate her options.

"Yes, Kia, Mr. Gilbert may be the answer. Perhaps I should transfer ownership to him and take a small share of the future proceeds from sugar cane sales to keep the church afloat." She smiled. "I look forward to teaching you, Kia, such an eager pupil makes for rewarding work. I wish I knew how much of what I say to you is understood. Very little, I suspect."

"Kia make tea." Her brilliant white teeth flashed, and Elizabeth believed everything would work out. *God's will be strong.* Would He abandon her in her time of need? She hoped He wouldn't, even though God would know all about her immoral thoughts.

As Kia was gathering the water for the tea, Elizabeth stood and led her to John Allen's room. Rebecca had stripped the bed and replaced the sheets with new ones. She had quietly taken care of that for Elizabeth, and Elizabeth was grateful for that small kindness. She pointed to Kia and then to the bed. "This will be your room now."

The large feather mattress was a true exorbitance in comparison to the beds stuffed with dried plantain leaves. To have two such luxuries was almost unheard of, and only the most prosperous had brought these items with them. The feather tick stuffed with goose down sat on top of an under mattress made of the more common plantain leaves. Of the two beds, her father's mattress was more comfortable as the stuffing was nearly double that of Elizabeth's.

Kia vigorously shook her head, and her eyes opened wide with fright. "No, Kia stay, Elizabeth."

Believing that Kia feared catching yellow fever from the bedding, Elizabeth soothed her. "Shhh, shhh. I won't make you sleep there, yet."

She wasn't sure how long she could resist touching the soft skin of Kia's shoulder, hips and other parts of her body, but Kia's comfort and sense of safety was more important to Elizabeth. She would resist the temptation. The devil was at work, and she would pray more for strength. The fortitude to resist. Her God would not let her down in her time of need.

†

The tiny line in Elizabeth's forehead appeared all too frequently, and Kia could not resist trying to smooth it out. She liked touching Elizabeth. Sometimes she would do this in the middle of the night, when Elizabeth tossed and turned. The tiny wrinkle would appear, and Kia knew that demons haunted her. When she would finally settle, Kia would move close and wrap her arm around Elizabeth's middle. She would breathe in the faint smell of soap, combined with the unique aroma of the pleasant looking woman.

Kia knew that Elizabeth enjoyed the touch of Kia's hand moving lightly over her hip, even though she pretended to remain asleep. Her breathing would change, and that's how Kia would know she was awake.

This morning, Elizabeth sighed before she carefully slipped out of bed. Kia caught her staring down at her, before she sat up in bed. Kia was perplexed when Elizabeth looked away in embarrassment. Her face was an open book, Kia could read her moods as easily as the clouds in the sky announcing an angry gale.

She'd understood when Elizabeth had tried to move her to the sick room. She also understood that Elizabeth thought she was frightened about the possibility of catching yellow fever if she slept in the sick bed. The real fear was that Elizabeth would push her away and no longer allow the touching she craved.

"Elizabeth teach Kia more words." Kia broke the awkward silence and teased a smile from the subdued woman.

"Yes, and someday you will read and write, Kia. Teaching is something I can do."

†

Rebecca groaned as she sat. She hoped the baby would arrive soon, because Abraham and the others were depending on her. Her husband wore a constant face of worry, and she feared the drought and pests were taking their toll on the crops. He took the weight of responsibility on his own broad shoulders, especially after John Allen's passing.

Cissy had come to help with the morning chores and was chattering away as usual. Rebecca's attention was elsewhere, until she heard her say something that caused an uncomfortable chill to her spine. She needed to have Cissy repeat the story.

"Tell me again what you heard outside of Smith's Tavern." Rebecca lifted her eyes and bore her gaze into Cissy.

"Mr. Mitchell say Miss Allen has an unnatural fascination with Kia." Cissy took great care in enunciating every word. Of late, she was attempting to sound more like Kia. Her own enchantment with the beautiful African was evident to Rebecca. Rebecca understood the appeal of intimacy between women. She'd had her own experiences before Abraham made his intentions known. The plantation owners tended to look the other way when the African women sought comfort from one another. The relaxed view did not extend to the refined British women, due to the shortage of unmarried women. The scarcity often resulted in mixed-race weddings that were of great debate and cause for a certain amount of scandal.

"What else did you hear, Cissy? Did Mr. Mitchell make any threats?"

"He talked of Anne Bonny and Mary Read and their trials. They was sentenced to hang." Cissy put her hands to her throat and stuck out her tongue in a grotesque mimicry of hanging.

"Cissy, do not retell the story of their hanging to the children."

"No, ma'am, I won't."

"I've heard the story of the female pirates. He did not suggest they were hung for their unnatural acts, did he?"

"I don't know, ma'am. He chased me away when he saw me hanging around."

"Am I unnatural, Miss Rebecca? I like to gaze on Miss Allen and Kia, and Captain Blythe has pretty, blue eyes."

"Best not to say that out loud in front of Mr. Clarke or Mr. Mitchell. Best not to say it out loud to any of the gentlemen who frequent the tavern."

"Yes, ma'am," Cissy answered. "Can I go see Miss Allen, now for my lesson? She is teaching me to speak better and read," she said with excitement.

CHAPTER EIGHT

Two weeks had passed since her father was buried, and Elizabeth was sitting at the solid wood table with *The New England Primer* open to Kia's eager eyes. Elizabeth wasn't sure how many of her words Kia understood, but she decided to begin the reading lessons at the same time Kia was learning to speak English. This proved to be a surprisingly good strategy, as Kia's sharp mind absorbed her teachings quickly.

"Adam," Kia recited with precision.

"Very good, Kia. Yes Adam, for A. *In Adam's fall, We sinned all.*" She patted Kia's arm lightly. Kia responded best to short sentences of praise followed by a reiteration of the lesson and a light touch to her arm or hand. Elizabeth passed off this practice as leveraging the potency of human connection. Although she had always been taught to keep a proper distance, hugging and touch was offered freely by the natives. Elizabeth had lost some of her stiffness since moving to Antigua two years ago.

The loud knock on the door startled Elizabeth. After she opened the door, she suspected her surprise must have been evident on her face, as the red-faced overseer, George Mitchell, stood grinning at her.

"Miss Allen, I do apologize for showing up at your doorstep without a proper invitation. I wanted to pay my respects after your father's passing and to discuss an urgent matter with you." George blinked and stared at Elizabeth with an expression she thought looked like a grotesque amalgamation of smugness and a leer.

Elizabeth was tempted to drop the respectful address and call him George, but she feared the informality would lead him to believe there existed a certain familiarity between the two of them. That might give him a reason to try to court her. "Mr. Mitchell, you are two weeks late. I don't believe I saw you in the procession." She turned to Kia. "Kia, please wait in the other room for me. This won't take long."

George narrowed his beady eyes at Kia, as she walked into their bedroom. "You let your negro lie with you?"

"How dare you question my morals? She has a fear of the sick bed, and I'll not have her sleep on the floor like an animal. We do not see eye to eye on the treatment of the stolen Africans," she replied icily.

"Now why would you think I was questioning your morals, Miss Allen? I was merely surprised that you have not only taken this negro into your home, but you apparently lie next to her, as well. I thought that was merely scandalous talk without merit."

"The business, Mr. Mitchell. I've no time for idle chat."

"Ah yes, well, as you may know, or perhaps not, since you've left the running of your plantation to your other Negro, Abraham—"

"Mr. Gilbert is not my African. He is a free man, owned by no one."

"Right, right. I see. Well, the drought has created an almost untenable position for us, and now we have cause for an even graver concern, with the borer ravaging the crop. Surely, your man Abraham has informed you of this pest."

"Mr. Gilbert has informed me of the yellow blast, and I do believe we are managing to keep the insect from eradicating our crop. Your point, Mr. Mitchell." Elizabeth did not offer the disagreeable man a seat at her table, wishing their conversation would end quickly and she could return to her lessons with Kia.

"As you may know, Mr. Clarke is a generous man and has authorized me to make an offer to purchase your plantation, including a provision for the Negroes working your land. We can provide lodgings and food for these unfortunate free slaves, once their means of employ no longer exists. None are tradesmen, and Mr. Clarke does not wish for them to starve due to their change in circumstance."

"Get out," Elizabeth ordered through gritted teeth. "You may inform your employer that I would prefer to lose every last cane to the pests than sell the plantation to him."

"Hmmf. I should have known that a woman such as yourself, who does business with the likes of Captain Blythe, would act in an undignified manner. I had hopes that, as a woman of God, you would not have let her influence you. Mr. Clarke was only offering a solution, since you appear to rebuff all the advances of the gentlemen on the island who are willing to save you from the spinster's life and certain ruin of your plantation. I wash my hands of what will surely become of you."

"Good day, Mr. Mitchell. You have my answer, and it will never change." Elizabeth turned away, leaving her guest to see his way out. After the door closed, the air in her lungs released. She leaned on the heavy door.

Abraham's furrowed brow, as he talked about the destructive moth, had worried her. The voracious borer was perforating the rind of the plant. If they did not attend to the pest quickly, any crops they managed to save would be substandard and would not bring top dollar. Abraham had suggested an attempt to burn off the infected pieces. She had only nodded her assent, but her worry remained for the livelihood of all those families who depended on this crop for their survival.

Elizabeth failed to stop her tears. Suddenly, Kia was there, wrapping her arms around Elizabeth, hugging her closely, and stroking her back in a loving manner. Elizabeth knew she should break away from the young woman, but instead, she welcomed the velvety touch.

"Good to send bad man away," Kia murmured into her neck, as she continued to hold Elizabeth.

Elizabeth reluctantly took a step back, creating space between herself and Kia. "Yes, but at what cost? I do hope I have made the right decision."

"Abraham help Elizabeth. I help Elizabeth." Kia fingered the small curl of hair flopping against her temple, then let her finger trail down Elizabeth's face. Her boldness took Elizabeth by surprise, as she traced the outline of Elizabeth's lips before taking her hand and leading her back to the table. "Read book now."

†

Abraham organized the field workers to come together as one and burn the pest from the infected parts of the tall stalk. They managed to salvage a good portion of the crop. Elizabeth only hoped those efforts would bring in enough money to survive another year of drought and pestilence, should the next year prove as challenging. Abraham was surely sent by God himself to help her, as she struggled to maintain the plantation.

She wondered why the British had decided to try their hand at sugar cane with so many obstacles in their path. As she looked outside, she noticed the wind beginning to blow with the force of a hurricane. She hoped that Abraham was able to convince the workers to seek refuge inside their stone huts, even though the thatched roofs were often the first to go in the strong winds. She was well aware of the instances when man and horse, unable to keep their footing, had been blown down a precipice and expired as a result of what the natives called angry puffs. They did not seem like puffs of air to Elizabeth, but maybe God was reminding them of his displeasure.

Kia joined her at the window. Her frightened eyes caused Elizabeth to place her arm around Kia's shoulder, pulling her in close.

"Come. The bedroom will be safe. The winds will rattle the house, but it has withstood much worse." Elizabeth said those words out loud to appease Kia who had not been through this kind of storm. She hoped her words would prove true. The tempest was not merely a tropical storm but a full-fledged hurricane. At least the storm brought much needed rain, but at what cost to their livelihood—the precious sugar cane?

†

Kia was frightened by the rage of Mother Nature blowing outside, but Elizabeth had allowed a rare closeness that had never before occurred in broad daylight. Kia enjoyed nights spent with Elizabeth. In the cloak of darkness, Elizabeth sometimes allowed Kia's fingertips to graze over the cotton night frocks she insisted they both wear. Once, Kia had awoken to Elizabeth's hand caressing her face, and she wondered if she was dreaming. When Kia opened her eyes, Elizabeth had quickly separated herself from the welcomed closeness of their two bodies and jumped from the bed as if the feather tick was infested with vermin.

Today, Kia and Elizabeth were huddled together on the bed, and Kia felt Elizabeth's protective arms circled around her body. Elizabeth had brought her lips to Kia's forehead, and the soft pressure caused a pleasant tingle.

"You're safe, Kia," Elizabeth whispered, as she stroked Kia's back.

Kia clutched Elizabeth, molding her body against the woman. She wanted to feel the brush of her mouth on other parts of her body. As Kia's head rested on top of Elizabeth's breast, she ventured a tentative touch to her side, beneath the arm wrapped around her body. Elizabeth's trembling disturbed Kia, and she wanted to settle her in the same manner that Elizabeth was effecting with her tender caress.

When Elizabeth did not pull away, Kia emboldened her touch and brought her mouth to Elizabeth's neck. At first Kia misunderstood the groan followed by a small shudder, until she pulled back and feasted on Elizabeth's blissful appearance. She understood the earlier tremors now and boldly placed her lips firmly on Elizabeth's.

For a few glorious seconds, Elizabeth returned the intimate joining of their mouths and parted slightly to let Kia's tongue enter inside. Sucking gently on the fleshy part of her lower lip, Kia felt a surge of emotion. The feeling was short-lived. Elizabeth pushed Kia away as if her very mouth was set aflame like the infested sugar cane.

"No, Kia. We must not allow the devil inside."

Kia could not mask the hurt from Elizabeth's rebuff, and Elizabeth's response was quick as she gathered her back into her arms. "Shhh. This is not your fault. I am to blame; for my spirit might appear strong, but my flesh is weak."

Kia felt the moisture on Elizabeth's cheeks and brought her hands to Elizabeth's face to wipe the tears away. "Love is good, Elizabeth. Strong not weak."

Elizabeth sighed, as she brought her forehead to rest against Kia's. "We can seek comfort in one another during the storm, but we must resist the temptation of the flesh."

CHAPTER NINE

The storm passed. The roof was repaired and sugar cane salvaged, but Elizabeth could not exorcise the memories of the afternoon spent in Kia's arms and the forbidden kiss. She had prayed every day for God to take away her feelings, to heal her sickness. Her feelings had not lessened one bit. In fact, every day, her love for Kia intensified.

Elizabeth was no longer under any illusion about who or what she was. Despite the teachings of her church, she had fallen from grace and given in to the perversity. Perhaps her brief mistake would be forgiven but not her continued licentiousness, as her emotions expanded. She wondered if he would judge her harshly for her evolving acceptance of her unnatural tendencies. She began to question why loving another human being was so wrong.

Elizabeth might be able to avoid temptation, but she could never give up her love for Kia. The beautiful African was the sustenance she needed to survive, like the very air she breathed in or the food and water she put in her body.

In her effort to justify her nature, Elizabeth began to scour the Bible for passages proving her love as pure and good. Perhaps the buggery laws were only intended for the men. Although there were whispers of unnatural women, she had never heard of a conviction ending in a hanging or life imprisonment. Those were limited to the men.

Despite her growing acceptance of this fundamental flaw, she knew this love must be hidden at all costs. George Mitchell would like nothing better than to declare her unwell in an effort to expand his employer's holdings and consequently line his own pockets.

Kia was out tending their small garden. Her affinity for encouraging the small shoots to climb to the sky brought a healthy bounty of fresh food to their table. Leaving the management of the sugar cane to Abraham and the other free Africans allowed Elizabeth to spend all of her time teaching the children.

The joy that burst from Elizabeth when teaching and working side by side with Kia was hard to contain. Her smile widened when Kia brought the newly harvested vegetables inside in the folds of her skirt.

"Miss Rebecca is on her way with the baby," Kia announced.

"Oh dear, I have been remiss in my duties. I should have gone to her hut instead." Elizabeth opened the door and ushered Rebecca inside, as she cooed at the small bundle.

"Meet John Gilbert," Rebecca said with pride.

Tears glistened in Elizabeth's eyes. "You named him after my father." She reached out to touch his tiny fingers.

"Yes, a strong name for a fine man. He will be as great a man as his namesake. You will teach him to read and write."

"Of course. Come sit." Elizabeth gestured to her table.

Rebecca's face grew grim. "Mr. Mitchell is stirring up scandal again. He is trying to sway the marshal and the magistrate that you should not be allowed to retain your plantation because of your refusal to marry and your unnatural affection for Kia."

Elizabeth frowned. She suspected George Mitchell would not take kindly to her abrupt refusal of his offer. Kia was quietly preparing tea, and Elizabeth murmured, "Thank you, Kia."

"Sell the lands to Mr. Gilbert," Kia interjected.

"We do not have money to purchase your plantation," Rebecca relayed in misery.

Elizabeth was surprised by Kia's words and thought them brilliant. "Surely you can afford to pay one pound."

Rebecca looked up. "You cannot sell your plantation for a pound. Abraham is a proud man, he would never accept that indenture. Mr. Allen already made a generous provision for us in his will."

"I don't need or want the plantation. Father left me well cared for. I can ask the solicitor to prepare a legal document that will provide for a small percentage of the profits in exchange for the undervalued price of the land. I suspect there will be nothing Mr. Mitchell can do to challenge the legality. I am not without my own allies."

Elizabeth stood and gathered Kia in her arms hugging her tightly. "You are brilliant, Kia."

Kia seemed to bask in the glory of Elizabeth's praise, as she looked at her with such love in her eyes.

A tiny smile appeared on Rebecca's face. "A most ingenious solution."

Elizabeth had a sudden burst of hope. The fat overseer might deem the plan devious, but Elizabeth now understood the power of bringing together women who could think differently than a man. For women, it was not about competition or conquering another but about collaboration, so that all parties share in the prosperity. Later, she would worry about the other component to his claims, which unfortunately, were not without merit. Her affection for Kia did extend beyond that of friendship or concern for her everlasting life and sharing the word of God.

†

The light knock on the door was expected. Elizabeth suspected she might need to help Abraham understand her reasoning without harming his considerable pride. Although he would never speak ill of her, she sensed his discomfort, unlike his wife, who seemed to inherently understand the nature and depth of Elizabeth's relationship with Kia.

"Mr. Gilbert, thank you for coming to discuss the urgent matter. Please, sit down and let me offer a proposal that I believe will suit both of our needs."

Abraham stepped awkwardly inside and remained standing, until Elizabeth insisted he sit. He pulled the hat from his head. "Rebecca told me of your plans, Miss Allen and—"

"Will you please hold your objections until I explain my rationale?"

Abraham nodded, but sat rigid in the chair.

"If I do not sell to you quickly, Mr. Clarke and Mr. Mitchell will use every imagined indiscretion to force my hand. If he manages to catch the ear of the magistrate, who is sympathetic to Mr. Clarke, not only my good reputation will be lost, but your own livelihood will be at risk. Mr. Mitchell's contrivance includes an offer of indenture not much different than ownership with the paltry amount he would pay you. I cannot allow that to happen and dishonor the memory of my father. I will sell the plantation for the sum of one pound. In exchange, you will pay me ten percent from the net proceeds on the sale of the sugar cane."

"Twenty," Abraham countered.

"Done. I shall have my solicitor draw up papers in haste."

"Miss Allen. I do not know how to thank you. Mr. Mitchell is an evil man. What he is saying to his friends about you and Miss Kia is abominable. I do not presume to understand, but I know you are a fine woman with impeccable morals."

"Mr. Gilbert, your vocabulary is improving. Have you been reading the books I loaned to you?" Elizabeth teased.

His gleaming smile was his answer. "Perhaps someday, I will leave the fields for the pulpit."

"Father would be pleased by that. I do believe if he could have had a son, he would have been proud to call you his own."

If Abraham decided to preach, he would need to find a replacement to run the plantation. She wondered if someday his son would take over. Even though ten acres was a small plantation, too many depended on Abraham to feed their own families, and she would never wish for him to sell to Mr. Clarke. Yet, how could she discourage his passion for spreading the word of God to others? This was a conundrum she hoped would never come to pass.

✝

Samuel Barlow, the solicitor, was a kindly, refined gentleman in his late forties. His full head of silver hair was tied neatly and hung on the nape of his neck. He brought with him a clerk to help transcribe Elizabeth's wishes. She was surprised to see the clerk was a young African man of about twenty-five, who looked upon Samuel as lovingly as she suspected her furtive glances at Kia might appear to others. Having experienced love for the first time, she understood all the symptoms. Yes, symptoms, because love felt like a sickness to her.

Her father had always spoken highly of Mr. Barlow. As a prominent member of the elite in Antigua, his opposing views on slavery carried some weight with the magistrate and a minority of the elite. Yet, the majority would look the other way at the harsh treatment of slaves. Many of the plantation owners believed it was less expensive to replace a field worker expiring from exhaustion than to care for their slaves properly. Mr. Barlow's orations about the mistreatment of slaves were well known.

With a small bow, Mr. Barlow entered the modest dwelling with his clerk in tow. "Good Morning, Miss Allen." He removed his hat. "May I present Mr. William Barlow, my clerk."

Elizabeth raised her eyebrow. "Surely you have not taken a slave to assist in your office, Mr. Barlow."

"No, no, nothing of that sort. William requested a change in his surname to match my own. He is a bright lad with great promise. I hope he will continue to study law and take my place one day. He is quite capable of recording your wishes."

"Would you like some tea...oh dear, it sounds quite humorous to say Mr. Barlow and Mr. Barlow." Elizabeth stifled a laugh.

"It does, indeed. Yes, I believe both of us would very much appreciate a cup, if it is not too much trouble, Miss Allen. William?"

"Yes, Miss Allen. Thank you, I would appreciate some tea," William's deep voice answered.

Elizabeth noticed Kia's keen eyes taking in the interchange and the familiarity between William and Samuel. "We can conduct business in the parlor."

"Let me prepare the tea for you," Kia offered.

"Ah, this lovely woman must be Kia. Your English is very precise. Elizabeth must be a great teacher."

"She is, Mr. Barlow." Kia's eyes sparkled.

Samuel laid a piece of parchment, quill pen, and a traveling ink well on the ornately carved wooden table, the other luxury Elizabeth allowed herself.

"Shall we begin, Miss Allen? What business do you wish to record?"

"I wish to sell my plantation to Mr. Gilbert for the sum of one pound," Elizabeth directed.

Samuel arched his eyebrow and glanced at William. "That is an unusual sum."

"There is more to the proposition. In exchange for the low sum, Mr. Gilbert has agreed to pay me twenty percent of the net profits."

"Ah, I see now. I do believe you found a way to turn the tables and not allow Mr. Clarke the upper hand." Samuel laughed heartily, and William's lips curved in mirth.

"It was Kia who offered this solution, and a brilliant one it is, indeed," Elizabeth remarked.

Kia brought the teapot to the table, setting it next to the ink well. She hurried to gather three cups and placed them on the table next to the pot. Elizabeth glanced up at Kia and smiled. "Kia, are you not having tea? Please, come and join us," she encouraged.

The joy on Kia's face was Elizabeth's just reward for the invitation. "Mr. Barlow, will you please draw up the papers so that there are no loopholes. I do not wish to debate this in court."

"I assure you, Mr. Clarke shall have no reason to challenge this document. I still have considerable influence, and I shall make sure of it."

Seeing Samuel and William together, she understood the nature of their relationship. Why hadn't she recognized that which was so obvious to her now? She wondered if he had endured the taunt of twiddle poop. She'd heard that once or twice and asked her father what it meant. He'd said it was a term some of the more uncivilized men used for an effeminate looking fellow and shook his head in disgust. Perhaps, her father would not be as disappointed in Elizabeth as she thought. As she remembered his reaction to the slur, she had renewed hope his sympathies and compassion had extended to those poor unfortunate souls with unnatural feelings. *Would he approve or look the other way?*

An epiphany flowed over Elizabeth, as she understood; if a person belonged to the elite class, many things were overlooked. Prosperity had a way of ensuring that even the men and women of God ignored sin, in exchange for monetary support. Over the years, Samuel had provided generous support to the church, and his charitable giving bought blindness and deafness from others.

After her guests left, Elizabeth let out the breath she was holding. With the business of the plantation complete, she could return to the church and the children who depended on her for their learning. Kia was coming along so well; Elizabeth could easily see her assisting in the future. She relished working side by side with Kia.

†

Kia had been pleased to sit and have tea with Samuel and William. In her brief time with the two men, she believed them to be good and kind gentlemen. She knew in her heart, those two men likely shared the same feelings Elizabeth was fighting. Why did Elizabeth not push them away or warn them?

As Kia read some of the Bible passages, her confusion amplified. She did not understand how her feelings for Elizabeth could be unnatural. They did not feel unnatural to her. The Bible only spoke of men who lie with one another as abominations. Elizabeth was not one to dwell on those passages, becoming uncomfortable when Kia asked her questions.

Kia looked curiously at Elizabeth when she heard the air expel from her mouth and loudly punctuate her mood. "Samuel Barlow and William Barlow share the same last

145

name as if they were married. They love each other," she stated.

"You must not repeat that, Kia. There are grave consequences to giving voice to your observations. These things are ignored, and we must do the same."

"I do not understand. They do not appear to be abominations to me. Their appearance is pleasant, and their kindness leaks out like the water through the Barbados stone. Perhaps the evil is trapped in the same manner and renders their feelings pure, but how? I wish to find this sieve."

"My beautiful Kia," Elizabeth stroked her cheek. "I do wish it were that simple."

"Love is simple. Is it not? And pure. I do not believe it is anything but good," Kia responded.

"Perhaps you are correct, and there are some passages in the Bible that we do not fully understand. We should walk to the church now. The children love when you read to them. I am very proud of you," she praised.

"I love the children. Since I will not marry and have any of my own, this time with them is enough."

"Why will you not marry?"

"If slaves are not allowed to marry, why should I? If I marry, I would have to leave you, and I cannot do that. You have decided not to take a husband. Why should I not follow you?"

Elizabeth pulled Kia into an embrace. "Oh, Kia. I am so selfish, but must admit I am pleased with your decision."

"I will stay with you always." To Kia this was an easy declaration to make. She could not ever see herself leaving Elizabeth to stand beside another.

CHAPTER TEN

Weeks turned into months, and Elizabeth continued to wrestle with her feelings and the furtive touches at night. She wasn't sure if Kia's increasingly brazen behavior was as a result of her own evolving acceptance of her innate tendencies, or if the cover of darkness provided those few short hours of bliss she eagerly welcomed.

Neither had repeated the kiss. Although Elizabeth was desperate for Kia's lips, she knew that to cross that barrier would mean she was lost forever. Instead, Kia's hands would move across her body in the middle of the night, stroking everywhere but those most private places. Elizabeth had at least had the fortitude to stop Kia when her hand roamed too close to her breast or began the descent to the top of her pleasure center. On each occasion, her hips had lifted as praying hands might reach in the air for greater

147

effect. But before Kia reached the triangle of hair, Elizabeth would place her own hand on top and move it to a safer location.

Elizabeth could not stop the trickle of moisture that seemed to collect when Kia danced along the edges of what Elizabeth allowed. Nor could she hide the hitch in her breath any more than when Kia would react to her own explorations.

Elizabeth, too, had become more audacious in her transgressions. The intimacy of her feather light touch to Kia's face, tracing the outlines of her lips, and bringing the tips of her fingers to her neck and collarbone. Kia's neck and the hollow between the protrusion of bone was exquisite. Elizabeth was careful to avoid touching the darker circle around her nipple that she'd seen when helping Kia bathe when she first arrived. If her hand got close, she knew she would not be able to resist running her fingers along the outside of the darker-colored ring, as if sketching a picture. Her burgeoning need extended to an almost painful desire to take the nipple into her mouth and suckle. That thought both repulsed and excited her.

Elizabeth knew these urges were becoming increasingly difficult to stop. She craved the relief that only Kia's touch would provide. The yearning to bring their mouths together again was nearly impossible to ignore and took Elizabeth a great deal of effort every night they lay side by side. She could not bear to suggest that Kia sleep in her father's room, so she continued to endure the torture. *Perhaps this is my penance.*

Elizabeth forced herself to think of other things this morning, as the sun was near to rising. Today, Kia would teach her first lesson to the children. She would read the story of Adam and Eve.

As her fingers skimmed over Kia's arm, the warm brown eyes opened. "Good morning, Elizabeth."

Elizabeth smiled. "Good morning. Are you ready for today?"

Her bright-white teeth glimmered in the predawn darkness. "Yes. I would like to show you a passage, Elizabeth. I have thoughts about the meaning."

Kia had studied every passage in the Bible, committing her favorite sections to memory. Elizabeth was so proud of her declaration that she wished to become a minister, and took her seriously. The great John Wesley himself had authorized Sarah Mallet to preach, despite the objections of the male ministers. Perhaps Kia might make history as the first African woman to share the word of the Lord.

Reluctantly, Elizabeth pushed the light cover aside and stretched, breaking contact with Kia. "I will make the tea for us this morning, and perhaps we can eat some of that fine rum cake you brought back from Rebecca."

"Oh yes. That would be lovely," Kia answered.

†

As Elizabeth and Kia sat at the large table drinking their tea and nibbling on the cake, Kia opened the well-turned pages of the King James Bible to the book of Ruth. "Will you read this passage and help me unravel the lesson? I wish to understand Ruth 1:16." Kia pointed to the passage.

Elizabeth smiled. She knew she should not be surprised by Kia's question. She'd turned to that passage and speculated on the underlying meaning herself. In her greatest despair, she had grasped for straws to try to find a different interpretation to the early teachings of the church. Before her mother passed, she had cautioned Elizabeth to avoid too much familiarity with her childhood companions. Even as a young girl, she knew her infatuations were not normal.

Elizabeth didn't know why she hadn't been brave enough to ask her father about the story of Ruth and Naomi. He died so suddenly; she never had the chance to seek his counsel. She wiped the tear from her eye, as she thought of her dear departed father.

"Elizabeth, what has caused your sadness?"

"I was thinking of my father and how he would have known the answer to your question."

"I regret not making his acquaintance. I believe that Ruth loved Naomi as I love you. I never wish to part from you, even in death." Kia closed the distance between herself and Elizabeth and brought their lips together for the briefest instance. The kiss could not be considered lustful, and yet it was not innocent either. Just a hint of intimacy and something more in but a flutter of time. Elizabeth did not rebuff Kia.

"Kia, we must find a way to ensure our bodies rest side by side in death. I know the graves of the British do not lie with the graves of Africans, but there must be a way. I cannot abide us being apart, as you have already said—even in death."

This was the closest Elizabeth would come to admitting her love for Kia, and yet, she knew the words did not need saying for Kia to understand her feelings. That awareness had been there almost from the start, from the very instant their eyes locked together. Light and dark riveted to one another. She wondered if she said the words out loud, that she loved Kia, if a terrible fate would follow for both of them.

CHAPTER ELEVEN

Kia was in a glorious mood. In the previous evening, when she had moved close to Elizabeth in the middle of the night, Elizabeth had turned to face Kia and allowed their bodies to mold together. She could feel Elizabeth's ample bosom against her own, with a scant slip of light cotton between them. She had wrapped her legs around Elizabeth's, and her body began to move of its own volition. Elizabeth began to rock along with her, and a strange sensation overtook her body, as her center heated against Elizabeth's thigh.

Kia boldly clutched Elizabeth's backside, holding her close, and Kia knew the moans that escaped Elizabeth's lips were not cries of pain but rather the same pleasure that overcame Kia. A kind of tension built inside, then exploded. She shook and trembled from deep in her core. When

Elizabeth cried out her name, Kia believed the shudder against her rigid leg was the same feeling. She fell asleep wrapped in Elizabeth's protective arms, as a kind of peace swept over her.

Elizabeth blushed when she woke that morning but did not pull away. They lay together basking in their love.

✝

Cissy knocked on the door, eager to share the town scuttlebutt. Normally, Elizabeth would stop Cissy from embellishing, but this morning she allowed her to chatter on as they drank their tea.

"Mr. Mitchell is still complaining loudly about you selling your land to Mr. Gilbert. He vowed to fix you. He whips his slaves without reason every chance he gets, claiming they are lazy and not working fast enough. You best watch your Ps and Qs," Cissy said. "I heard he paid Mr. Dougherty four bits to give one of the slaves a double whipping in the public square today."

Elizabeth turned her head, and the pain on her face was heartbreaking to Kia. "I was going to send you and Kia to town for supplies, but I suppose we can wait another day."

"We can take the long way and avoid the public flogging," Kia said.

Elizabeth frowned. "The men are always stirred into a frenzy after a whipping, we'll make do."

"I'm not afraid of that fat Mr. Mitchell. His face looks like a pig," Cissy declared.

"Cissy! That is not very Christian of you," Elizabeth admonished, as she covered her mouth with her hand in an attempt to hide her mirth.

Cissy linked her arm into Kia's and pulled her out the door. "We'll get the supplies like we do every week, Miss Allen. Come on Kia, you can help me carry them."

In addition to visiting the shop, they would be able to attend the Sunday market. Kia was getting used to the Sunday market and liked to arrive shortly after daybreak to have the best selection of poultry, fish, fruit, and vegetables. The first occasion she had to visit the market had overwhelmed her with the noise and smell. The loud jabber of the other Africans and squalling children basking in the sun, combined with the offensive aroma of bodies not used to regular bathing, had been difficult at first. Particularly harsh was the aroma of rotting food and stinking salt fish left on tables, putrefying to the final stages of decay. Kia never bought those items, knowing they could cause great sickness if consumed. On her return journey to the house after the market closed at three, Kia still retained the stink in her nostrils, nearly a quarter of a mile away. The stench was worse than a chamber pot.

†

When Cissy and Kia had not returned by midday, Elizabeth began to worry that something terrible had happened. Rum and public whippings were a dangerous combination, and she knew the overseers took pleasure in seeing the punishments carried out.

The severe punishments inflicted on slaves were often the topic of John Allen's sermons. Elizabeth thought she had left behind the well-known practice of the picket, but that form of torture and new barbarous inventions made their way to the island.

She had averted her eyes when a man, who had already been severely whipped, stood for hours on the flat top of the peg. She hurried away in disgust when listening to the men explain the excruciating pain caused by the thumbscrew. She couldn't imagine why fastening a person's thumbs together would create such agony, but the pain etched across the men's faces was a clear indication of the impact. Elizabeth could not bear to see the men and women chained together with their iron necklaces, and often avoided the journey to town altogether, preferring to send Cissy for supplies. Without reason other than to cause pain, the cruelest overseers added pot hooks to the neck collars. The bent hooks pointed outward preventing the slave from lying down their heads.

Abraham was breathing heavy when he pushed open the church doors. "Miss Allen, Kia and Cissy have been taken to jail. Mr. Mitchell claims they were found idling outside the merchant's general store. He called upon the marshal to place advertisements announcing them both as runaways."

Elizabeth stood and left her circle of bewildered children so that she could have a private conversation with Abraham. She pulled him to the side. "That's preposterous. He knows very well that neither are runaways." Elizabeth paced in agitation.

"Mr. Clarke has both a sympathetic magistrate and the marshal. It is rumored he lines their purses."

"I'd better call on my friend, Mr. Barlow. We will need all the assistance we can muster. I cannot let him do this."

Elizabeth had a brief thought that God was now punishing her for indulging in the pleasure of the flesh. Her confusion returned. After her discussion on the Book of Ruth, Elizabeth had begun to believe her love for Kia was not against God's laws. Her God was full of love and compassion, not spite and fury.

"I'll come with you."

"No, Mr. Gilbert. I cannot take a chance that Mr. Clarke or Mr. Mitchell has you in their line of sight. Please, stay here with the children. I'll settle this myself, even if I have to bring Captain Blythe back for that duel she promised."

Abraham smiled. "I would like to be witness to that myself."

Elizabeth gathered her skirts and ran to the harbor. She hoped that Mr. Barlow had enough influence with the other elite in town. Cissy would not be a problem, because Elizabeth knew her father had the proper papers drawn up to prove she was a freed slave, but Kia had no such papers. An oversight Elizabeth would need to correct. She only hoped it wasn't too late.

†

Kia and Cissy huddled in the corner of the cold, dark cell. The marshal leered at them, and she feared he would do more than look. His body odor reminded her of Sunday market, and she tried not to breathe in the stench. Memories of the slave trader shackling her and leading them into the small hold nearly overwhelmed her with fright, but she was a much stronger woman now. She thought of the salted herring, displayed side by side in the market—tiny little pieces of fish.

Kia didn't understand why she'd been jailed. She and Cissy weren't idle, and they weren't runaway slaves. They were simply waiting for the shopkeeper to put together the supplies. Holding her wits about her, she kept her eyes to the ground as she'd been taught when interacting with the white men. Kia knew Elizabeth would come for them.

The shopkeeper had roughly ordered them to wait outside and not stink up his shop. Not more than five minutes had passed, when the marshal cited the law allowing him to seize them and place them in the dank cell.

Cissy held Kia's hand. "Miss Allen will bring the papers to prove we are free. The marshal has to post runaways for two days to give the slave owners time to collect their slaves."

"There are no papers for me," Kia answered.

Cissy's eyes grew large. "Oh, Kia, what will we do to prove you are free? I can tell the magistrate that I saw Captain Blythe leave you under the care of the mission with Miss Allen, but they do not believe the Africans."

"Yes, I am aware of that. Have faith, Cissy. Elizabeth and God will find a way."

"God does not take care of us. Where is He when the men are whipped?" Cissy whispered in anger. Kia was surprised. She'd always thought Cissy was a happy young woman, content to tell her tall tales to the children. The underlying anger was something new. Kia suspected that before Cissy was free she'd endured a great deal of pain. Kia felt lucky that Captain Blythe had left her with Elizabeth. Sweet Elizabeth, whose arms she so longed to fall into.

The smells of human excrement and other noxious odors were overwhelming, and Kia could just make out movement of some creature in the dim light. She thought of how Cissy might spin a story of her experience in the cell, making the rats as big as cats and the cockroaches as large as her hand. These varmints carried disease, and she knew they would need to remain vigilant to keep the pests from nipping at their skin.

"Cissy, we must take turns to stay awake and keep the rats from biting." Kia stomped her foot and a curious rat scurried away.

"My eyes are wide open. I don't like rats." Cissy began to cry.

"Shhh, shhh, I will keep them away. Just think of the tales you'll be able to tell the children."

Cissy's tears began to slow, and she looked up. "I'm happy you are here with me."

A disturbance outside the stone walls garnered her attention. Elizabeth. She heard her speaking to the marshal. Her light tones had an edge of worry. Kia was settled by her presence, even though she knew her circumstance was bleak.

†

Elizabeth squinted into the sun and looked upon the small sign, Samuel Barlow, Solicitor. Her footsteps were hurried, as she made her way to his office. He would have a copy of the papers on Cissy and hopefully help her with documents for Kia.

Before she had a chance to knock or announce her presence, William opened the door and looked at her curiously. "Miss Allen, you look out of sorts. Please, come in."

Samuel stood, his face grave. "I was expecting you, Miss Allen."

"So, you've heard."

William looked perplexed. "Samuel?"

"The marshal took Miss Cissy and Miss Kia to the jail, after Mr. Mitchell paid the marshal a small sum. Hardly worth the aggravation, if you ask me. Mr. Mitchell is insisting they are both runaways and must be put to auction in two days if their owners do not claim them."

The sadness in William's eyes told Elizabeth everything she needed to know.

"I must see her and…" She slumped in the chair.

Samuel walked over and patted her hand. "I have the papers for Miss Cissy. We will be able to have her released, but Miss Kia will have to remain in the jail until the time of auction. How much of your inheritance are you willing to offer to settle this affair?"

"I would give every last shilling provided in my father's will to ensure Kia's safety. Just tell me what I need to do."

Samuel nodded. "I do not believe there has been enough time to defile—"

"Defile!" Elizabeth cried in anguish. "Please, Mr. Barlow, what can we do to keep this from happening?"

"I will loan you the silver until you can make arrangements with the bank. An offer of five pounds will be more than sufficient to allow you to see Miss Kia. We will offer double that amount to ensure he does not touch her. That is more than four months' salary for him and would be difficult to refuse. I believe it is also more than Mr. Mitchell offered to jail them." Samuel lifted his eyes to William who nodded and walked behind a large desk. He pulled a sturdy metal box from one of the drawers.

"Why not offer a greater sum to simply release them?"

"The notices have already been posted. It is too late for that now. I am sorry Miss Allen, but you will need to buy Miss Kia at auction."

Elizabeth gasped. "I cannot do that. Mr. Barlow, you know my beliefs on slavery."

"If you wish for Miss Kia to survive. I'm afraid you must."

"Will Kia ever forgive me?"

"She will, Miss Allen, she will. I've nothing but affection for Samuel, and he owned me for a brief time," William answered.

"I must see her and help her understand. The rats. How will we keep the rats from biting? I know all about those jails."

"Miss Kia is smart, she will know to keep the rats away," Samuel answered.

William handed Samuel a large purse that Elizabeth presumed was filled with silver. When Samuel tugged on her arm she steeled herself for what she needed to do.

✝

Elizabeth was clutching Samuel's arm, as she made her way to the stone building that sat next to the courthouse. She shuddered as she approached, and Samuel squeezed her arm. "I will offer the silver to the marshal."

"I understand. He would not look upon my offer too kindly. Women are not supposed to enter into business affairs. I suspect that is what instigated this situation. I had the audacity to sell my plantation to an African."

"I am afraid that is one of the reasons. The other is that Mr. Clarke has set his sights on Miss Kia and wishes to take her as his mistress."

Elizabeth was horrified at that prospect. She'd heard rumor of how brutally he beat his former mistress, who had mysteriously disappeared. Authorities refused to look into the situation. Another lost slave was not their concern. Cissy had told of him pouring boiling water down his mistress's throat as a form of punishment. Elizabeth wondered if the story could be true. Cissy said that was how the mistress died, and Elizabeth was now prone to believe the accuracy of the tale. It was not the first time she had learned of that punishment.

"I will bid my entire fortune if that's what it will take."

"I do not believe that will be necessary. Mr. Clarke is a miserly man and will not bid much above the going rate. A bid of fifty pounds will surely exceed any amount he would be willing to pay."

The marshal lifted his immense body from the chair when Elizabeth and Samuel entered. Elizabeth turned her head in disgust when he spat leaving an ugly brown glob on the floor. His yellow teeth appeared when he greeted the two visitors, "Mr. Barlow, what business do you have today? Surely those Negroes are not your slaves." His eyes narrowed in their direction.

"I have the papers to release Miss Cissy, proving she is a free slave, and offer a sum of five pounds for the inconvenience to you, as Miss Allen wishes to speak with Miss Kia."

The marshal's greedy eyes glanced at the purse Samuel held in his hand and made a gesture to accept the silver. "Yes, an inconvenience that deserves compensation."

"If Miss Kia is not harmed in any way during her time in the jail, I offer an additional ten pounds. I will take the word of Miss Kia over yours, and no payment will be provided if you have defiled her in any way."

"I do not defile the runaway slaves Mr. Clarke wishes to purchase, but I can allow certain provisions to ensure her stay is more comfortable."

"So, Mr. Clarke has already offered compensation?"

"Not nearly as great a sum as you are offering. I will keep the others away." His mouth widened to show brown specks on his crooked yellow teeth.

Samuel counted out five pounds and handed the silver to the marshal. "The rest will be paid when Miss Kia is released." He pulled a set of papers from his jacket and handed them to the marshal. "These are the papers to release Miss Cissy. I believe you will find them in perfect order. Now, please take Miss Allen to see Miss Kia, and release Miss Cissy."

"She will need to speak to her through the bars," the marshal amended.

Samuel nodded. With great difficulty, Elizabeth remained mute throughout the exchange. Intuitively, she understood not to make matters worse. She attempted to portray a weak and subservient woman. Of greatest import was ensuring that Kia was unharmed and letting her know of their plan so she was not surprised.

CHAPTER TWELVE

Two days had passed, and Kia was exhausted from remaining awake to keep away the biting rats. She kept replaying her conversation with Elizabeth, when the marshal had released Cissy and left her alone in the cell.

After Mr. Barlow led the marshal and Cissy away, Kia was able to look into Elizabeth's teary, blue eyes. There was such pain in them that Kia wanted to rip the bars away and hold her in her arms.

"My beautiful Kia, I came as soon as I could. I am to blame for this. It is my weakness that has caused God to punish us both."

Kia reached through the bars, and Elizabeth accepted her hands. "No, my love. God does not punish the faithful. Cruel men are responsible, not God. If God were punishing

163

men and women for their sins, don't you think the overseers and masters would feel the sting of a whip and not the slaves? You cannot believe this is the wrath of a loving God."

"What else am I to believe? After my unnatural thoughts as I bathed you, Father was taken away. Now, after I surrendered to the weakness of the flesh, you have been taken from me."

"I will never be taken from you. Even in death, I will remain with you always."

"Kia, I pray you will forgive me for what I must do." Elizabeth looked away, and Kia brought her hands to Elizabeth's face to return their gaze upon one another.

"Elizabeth, I know there is nothing you would ever do that would require forgiveness, but even if there was, I will always forgive you."

"I cannot stop your placement on the auction block in two days' time. The only choice I have is to bid on you myself. I will spend every last shilling to ensure…"

"I'm not worth it."

"Yes, you are, and so much more than I have to offer. Mr. Barlow will draw up the papers for your freedom. Immediately following purchase, he will record them, so they can never take you away from me again. But, Kia, you will be my slave for the briefest moment."

Kia smiled and whispered, "I would gladly be your slave, Elizabeth, for however long you wish."

Elizabeth kissed her fingers. "We have arranged with the marshal to ensure your safety. You must tell me if he or any other lays a hand on you."

Kia closed her eyes. "I will. Thank you, Elizabeth."

Kia could tell by the marshal's lascivious looks that he wanted to lay his hands all over her, but his greed won out. She sent a small prayer of thanks to both her Lord and Elizabeth for this miracle. She understood that others in her position did not fare as well.

The marshal's hands were on her body, as he led her to the auction block. She was finally free of the jail, but his hands had traveled over her body before the bright sunshine hit her eyes. She would not tell Elizabeth, because he had not done worse and if Elizabeth challenged him too much, she feared for them both.

The oil used to put a sheen on Africans and make them more appealing was brought out. A withering look from Elizabeth saved Kia from the humiliation, and she was allowed to keep her frock to cover her nakedness.

Mr. Clarke and other men were in the crowd, standing beside Elizabeth. Mr. Clarke licked his bulbous lips and called out, "Remove her dress. I need to see that her skin is unmarred."

"No!" Elizabeth shouted. "I bid fifty pounds without the need to remove her frock." She turned her attention to Mr. Clarke and stared at him with a coldness Kia had never seen.

"Fifty pounds! Surely you jest, she is not worth more than thirty." Mr. Clarke crossed his arms over his massive chest. "This is why women should not enter into the business of men. Do you even have that much in silver, Miss Allen?"

"I do, and unless you wish to bid more, I insist the auctioneer close the bidding."

The auctioneer looked from Elizabeth to Mr. Clarke. "Will you offer more, Mr. Clarke?"

He shook his head and walked away, muttering, "That imbecile George will pay me for the wasted shillings."

"Anyone else wish to offer a bid?"

The other men milling about dispersed, leaving Elizabeth and Mr. Barlow. "Very well, sold to Miss Elizabeth Allen for the sum of fifty pounds."

Kia could see Elizabeth breathe out and lower her head. When her eyes returned to Kia, she saw several tears travel down her cheeks. Kia smiled and looked to the sky. The sunshine and fresh breeze danced across her skin and she was free again.

†

Elizabeth searched Kia's body for any marks that would indicate she'd been injured. There was nothing obvious, but it was possible the punctures or bruises existed in a covered area. She lamented that she could not do anything about the scarring of her spirit. The mental anguish would never go away. The dark circles under Kia's eyes were all the evidence Elizabeth needed to tell her that Kia had not slept since being jailed. After bathing her again, she would tuck her into bed and soothe her with whispers of love and devotion.

She hurried to Kia and took her arm not caring who was observing her. "Mr. Barlow, I need to take Kia home now. I will be by tomorrow, to collect a copy of the papers proving her freedom."

Samuel nodded. "Of course, but that won't be necessary. We shall bring the papers to you. Do not fret. Even Mr. Clarke cannot undo this. I suspect, right about now, he is more disgusted with his overseer than you. He was led to believe that his meager offer of twelve shillings in addition to a purchase price for Kia would ensure ownership. I would not wish to be Mr. Mitchell right now."

"Thank you, Mr. Barlow, for all you have done. I don't know what I would have done without your assistance."

"Never forget that wealth has certain privileges, and do not be concerned about using them to your advantage. You can either feel guilty or recognize the power of that privilege to influence the plight of those less fortunate than yourself. True love is also something worthy of fighting for. I trust you won't forget that either. Good day, Miss Allen."

"Good day, Mr. Barlow." Elizabeth nodded in acknowledgement of his wise words. She hadn't thought of her inheritance in that way. The realization began to melt away the guilt, as she understood the meaning behind his words.

†

Elizabeth was trembling, as she began to lead Kia from the center of town. She was startled from her worry, when she heard a commotion near the wharf. She looked up to see George Mitchell huffing up the hill to meet Mr. Clarke and calling out his name. Mr. Mitchell's eyes went wide, and Elizabeth followed his gaze. She smiled when she saw the imposing figure of Captain Blythe step onto the weathered, wood planks with a grim expression on her face. A black patch covered one eye. Her purposeful strides took her to where the short, rotund overseer and Mr. Clarke had already begun a loud discourse over the loss of Kia. Elizabeth paused and took a step closer, wanting to listen to what the handsome captain might have to say about Kia and Cissy's shady incarceration. Elizabeth remembered the warning Captain Blythe had issued when she brought Kia and the other women and children. She wasn't sure how she'd heard the news, but she was grateful for any support to ensure this never happened again.

"I am quite surprised, Mr. Mitchell. You failed to heed my warnings." Captain Blythe's steely gaze turned to Mr. Clarke. "You need to control your overseer. I believe I made myself clear when I brought the Africans to this island. Mr. Mitchell knew they were not runaways."

"I am most displeased by the way that my overseer has handled the situation. I assure you Captain Blythe, he will be dealt with. I wish no trouble from you. Please accept my deepest apologies for this most unfortunate incident." Mr. Clarke bowed.

"I do hope you are a man of your word. I will be very displeased to be forced to sail here to settle matters that should never have transpired. I will take that as a personal affront to my honor, should you fail to control your overseer again. In my world, Mr. Clarke, the only way to settle a dispute of honor is with a pistol. I can assure you that neither you nor Mr. Mitchell possess as keen an eye as I do, with or without my patch. I only need one eye to shoot."

"You have my word, Captain Blythe. I do not wish to enter into a duel with you over a trivial matter such as this."

Captain Blythe nodded, then glanced at Elizabeth and Kia and winked.

Elizabeth wanted to wait for Mr. Mitchell and Mr. Clarke to leave, before approaching the captain to thank her, but she felt a sense of urgency to take Kia home. Although she needed to ensure Kia was bathed and cared for, she could not ignore how the captain had gone out of her way to lend her strength and support. The captain had not only managed to issue her stern warning but also forced Mr. Clarke to reimburse Elizabeth for the price paid to the auctioneer.

Captain Blythe asked gently, "How are you, Elizabeth?"

"I am fine, now that they have released Kia and I was able to purchase her."

The captain frowned. "I have half a mind to march up that hill and shoot both of them between the eyes. I am disgusted by this news. I wish I had come a bit earlier, so that you did not have to endure the jail or the auction block."

"How did you hear about this?" Elizabeth asked.

"Ah, it is my business to keep abreast of the comings and goings on all the islands. Sailors often relay messages to one another through the tales we tell on land."

Elizabeth noticed how Kia kept her eyes to the ground. Although she did not wish to be rude, Elizabeth felt the urge to take Kia home without delay. She pulled Kia close to her in a protective embrace. "You must forgive me, Captain, but I need to take Kia home now. She has been through a harrowing ordeal. I am very indebted to you for confronting Mr. Mitchel and Mr. Clarke. I wish I could invite you to share some tea…"

The captain waved her hand in the air. "Please, do not worry yourself. We cannot remain long on the island and have a lot to accomplish before setting sail again. Perhaps you shall find the time to visit me on Saint Lucia, where I have retired with Cecelia."

Elizabeth nodded. "Thank you for understanding. Perhaps we will find a way to visit someday."

✝

The walk to her home was slow. Kia was so quiet that Elizabeth feared there were invisible scars she could never mend. Her only consolation was when Kia lifted her face to the sun, then turned and smiled. There was such trust and love in her eyes, Elizabeth's heart nearly broke.

Elizabeth had indulged in a small vial of oil to add to the water—a minor expenditure given her wealth. She was determined to remove all memories of Kia's time in jail. During her visit with Kia, the rank smells had invaded her nostrils. She could not imagine enduring that filth for two days. The fragrance of the rose petals would surely do the trick.

Before making her way to the auction, she had poured fresh water into the basin and added a liberal amount of oil, letting the scent infuse the clear water. A soft cloth lay next to the sweet smelling liquid.

She fingered the drawstring of Kia's outer garment, far different from the rags she'd worn in their first encounter. Elizabeth began to remove layers, one by one. She cared for Kia, caressing her skin as she removed the dank clothing. When Kia stood naked in front of her, Elizabeth gently brushed her hand over Kia's body, checking for bite marks or other evidence that she had not come out of the confinement unscathed.

"You were not harmed?" she asked.

Kia shook her head.

As she began to bathe Kia, her nipples puckered and a small sound escaped. Elizabeth knew that sound and her reaction was nearly instantaneous. A small amount of moisture leaked through her petticoat. How she wanted to kiss Kia. Her desire blew over her like the winds of a hurricane, devouring everything in its path.

After bathing every inch of Kia's body, she led her to the bed and turned to gather a nightshirt. Kia reached up, and her beseeching eyes were Elizabeth's final undoing. Removing her many layers was no small task, but soon, Elizabeth stood completely undressed before Kia. Her vulnerability and weakness on display.

"You are so beautiful, Elizabeth."

"God help me, I cannot hold back my love for you anymore. It is bursting through my every pore."

"Your touch will chase away every painful memory of when we were separated. I am not afraid of loving you."

"Nor I of you. Our God cannot be so cruel as to put you in the center of my path and not allow me to love you," Elizabeth whispered.

Crawling into bed, Elizabeth brought their mouths together—tentative and slow at first. The waves grew with her passion, and soon their tongues knotted together like an intricate rope, twisting and turning. She couldn't stop, she wanted more. Kia kissed her back as if Elizabeth was the last drop of water to sprinkle upon her skin after a long drought.

All the years and incessant warnings from the church no longer existed, because far from an admonition of her unnatural tendencies, nothing had felt more right at this moment. As her body melted into Kia's and both women ventured into forbidden territory, there was nothing tawdry about how they moved together in the ultimate culmination of love. She no longer attempted to reconcile the sin with the purity. The sanctity of her love for Kia, and Kia's love for her, won out.

Elizabeth surprised herself when she was the first to take Kia's breast into her mouth. The supple skin pressed against her tongue as if it had been made for her mouth to suckle. Kia arched up to meet her, demanding more contact. Elizabeth's hands moved of their own volition, across Kia's belly, and with only a slight hesitation, her fingers found the warm folds. Elizabeth was mesmerized by their effect, as Kia arched again and groaned in apparent ecstasy. Head thrown back, Kia pushed against Elizabeth's hand until her fingers slipped easily into the opening. Kia moved her pelvis up and down, allowing those fingers to slide in and out.

Soon, Elizabeth completely lost herself in the need to taste between Kia's thighs, to let the velvety part of her tongue make contact with the silky folds she'd discovered with her fingers. She didn't have time to dissect how scandalous that thought was, because she was already moving her kisses down Kia's body.

In answer to her bold moves, Kia opened her legs wide, her petals uncurling. Elizabeth thought of the early dew she collected with her tongue as a young girl. When she made contact with Kia's tiny droplets, she knew nothing would ever compare to this moment of bliss. When using the cloth to bathe between Kia's legs, Elizabeth had felt her tremble with need. When her mouth kissed Kia's center, she knew she would again feel the tremors that had erupted three days ago, before Kia was arrested.

Elizabeth reveled in the sensation of her fingers inside, as her mouth licked and sucked along the folds and at the top, where a tiny button caused Kia to squirm and moan louder. Nothing was as sweet to listen to as when Kia cried out, "Oh Elizabeth, my love, Elizabeth." Her whole body shook, then settled back into the feather mattress. Kia pulled

Elizabeth to lie next to her and kissed her before asking, "May I touch you now and let my love seep inside like you have done to me?"

"Yes," Elizabeth breathed out. She would fight this no more. Any fighting she would do in the future would be a fight to protect her love.

†

After their fevered lovemaking, Kia and Elizabeth fell into a deep sleep. Forgetting about the outside world, neither would go back. They'd made their decision, and although they understood the potential consequences for their choices, neither was willing to give up the connection they both felt when allowing their bodies to come together. Love had blossomed slow and precise, similar to how Kia learned English.

Periodically during the day, one or the other would awaken and begin anew, indulging each other in new ways, as they learned what brought about the most pleasure. Yet nothing could compare to the first time Elizabeth felt as if they became one body, entwined together for all eternity—the first time when all clothing was removed and it was just their two bodies moving together in a perfect synchronous dance.

The knock on the door startled Elizabeth. She panicked, as she tried to put on the many layers of clothing required of a proper Englishwoman to receive visitors. Kia jumped from the bed and touched Elizabeth's arm. "I will go, not as much is expected of me." She hastened to dress and closed the door to the bedroom before making her way to the entrance.

Elizabeth listened to the murmured voices. She thought she heard Samuel Barlow speaking. She continued to add to her many layers and smoothed her skirt, before opening the door to her bedroom.

Samuel and William were both standing awkwardly in the parlor. Samuel bowed and William looked away in embarrassment. "Forgive me for coming by so late, Miss Allen, but I thought you would wish to have these papers as soon as possible."

"Oh dear, let me make some tea. I do not usually lie in during the day…"

"It's quite all right, Miss Allen. We've only come to deliver the papers. Come William, let us take our leave. The women are still recovering from their ordeal." Samuel handed her the parchment. "Might I suggest, Miss Allen, that if you are able to spare a sum of one hundred pounds, I may be able to line the pockets of the remaining magistrates and other officials to ensure neither of you have further troubles? Saint Lucia is a fair distance, and the good captain may not be able to sail to our small island quickly enough to…"

"Yes, yes of course. Please, make those arrangements. Thank you, Mr. Barlow. For everything."

"You are most welcome. Good day, Miss Allen, Miss Kia."

As Mr. Barlow turned to leave, Elizabeth called out, "Mr. Barlow, has Captain Blythe set sail yet?"

"No, I believe she and her small crew planned to remain on the island for the evening and set sail tomorrow. Why?"

"I would like to show my appreciation to you both, and to Captain Blythe and her crew. Perhaps you will take a message to her to have all of you come to the mission tonight for a meal."

"I would be delighted to accept the invitation, and I believe Captain Blythe and her crew would enjoy a home-cooked meal. Thank you, Elizabeth. We shall return in two hours."

After the men left, Elizabeth looked down at her dress and noticed it was on backward. "Oh dear, I am not completely put together."

Elizabeth and Kia giggled and returned to the bedroom to properly adjust their clothing.

CHAPTER THIRTEEN

Several years had passed since Kia was released from jail and Elizabeth had completely yielded to her desires and affection for Kia. The increasing number of slave revolts and tensions on the plantations strengthened Elizabeth's resolve not to let anything happen to Kia, Cissy, or Abraham and his family.

The weekly supply trips to town were difficult for Elizabeth. She was exposed to the horrors and punishments inflicted on slaves with little to no provocation. Head down, she avoided any contact. Although the smaller shop was never fully stocked, she refused to spend another shilling to line the pocket of the shopkeeper who had knowingly subjected Kia and Cissy to cruelties neither deserved.

Committed to the mission, Elizabeth and Kia continued to spread the Gospel and educate the free slaves.

Although Elizabeth and her father had always worked side by side with the Moravians, sharing a common mission, she found herself warming more to the Moravians' less rigid teachings.

†

Eager faces smiled at Kia, as she recited the story of Ruth, her favorite. Elizabeth loved to listen to Kia's precise but almost musical tones, as she read from a book or told a story from memory.

Cissy had mellowed and matured over the years. When bringing news of the town, there was not a rush to her speech or a drama beyond the true events. She insisted on remaining informed, going to the port despite Elizabeth's protests. Although, she was never comfortable purchasing supplies without Elizabeth to accompany her.

Elizabeth could tell that Cissy had big news, as she strode confidently into the church. The day was 21st April, 1798.

"Miss Allen, the council has passed The Amelioration Act. The plantation owners cannot use the iron necklaces, and are required to provide better rations to their slaves," Cissy said with excitement.

Elizabeth smiled. "That is good news. I do wish the council would go further and abolish slavery. I suspect this act is more in response to the uprisings than addressing the immorality of owning slaves."

"Slaves can become husband and wife, but not in the church, and the hours of work are now limited. The council ordered the plantation owners to build a new hospital for the slaves, and the owners are required to provide medical care."

"All fine developments, but Kia still cannot be laid to eternal rest beside me, as in the story of Ruth and Naomi. Why has this not been rectified?" Elizabeth asked bitterly.

Kia stood and brushed Elizabeth's arm, revealing her keen sense of Elizabeth's rising agitation as her strong beliefs leaked out. "Where my body lies is of no import, because my soul will remain by your side," Kia whispered. "This is progress, Elizabeth. We must embrace every movement forward."

Elizabeth smiled at her companion. Although there was no doubt they were lovers, she retained the small amount of deception, enabling her to place in different compartments the various aspects of her life. A separation of church and private life was the manner she had chosen. Kia preferred to interpret the verses in the Bible uniquely to suit her own needs. Neither tried to convince the other to change their perspective on the matter.

"Mr. Barlow sends his regards and wanted to thank you for your generous donation. He reports the monies will be put to good use for those still recovering from years of drought and other ravages to the cane. He warns not to give away too much of your inheritance, as he predicts you and Miss Kia will live to a very old age and will need those funds to survive," Cissy said.

Elizabeth laughed. "He makes those dire predictions every time I see him. Father left me well cared for, and I've no heir for my wealth. Why should I not give it away to those in need? Besides, I receive a tidy sum from Abraham's continued good fortune. He has the magic touch that I suspect others wish for. He is teaching his young son, and I do not fear for the future."

"May I read my new story to the children now? I promise there are no sea monsters, only dashing female captains who save the day." Cissy grinned.

"Has Mr. Manu brought any news of the captain? How are she and Miss DuPont faring on Saint Lucia? I do miss the stories that Mr. Page brought of the seas, they were far more appropriate than your retelling of them. He has taken a wife, has he not, and retired near Captain Blythe?" Elizabeth asked.

"I hear they are faring quite well, prosperous actually. I do wish Captain Blythe would visit." Cissy sighed, and Elizabeth caught the dreamy look on her face. She'd long suspected that Captain Blythe, Cecilia DuPont, and Cissy were like her, and that made her feel less alone. Of course there was Kia, her beautiful Kia. But to know others had the same unnatural stirrings, somehow this settled her even more. These women were good and honorable. That fact did not escape her.

"Perhaps we should secure passage on a ship one day and visit," Elizabeth offered.

"Oh, could we, Miss Allen, could we? I hear the slaves are free on Saint Lucia," Cissy stated.

Kia smiled and Elizabeth laughed at Cissy's continued infatuation. "Yes, that island appears to be more progressive than ours, but then again it is not controlled by the British. There is still a bit of unrest there. I believe it would be prudent to wait until everything settles. I don't believe the British have given up the possibility of regaining control. While that would be a sad situation for the freed slaves, travel to Saint Lucia will be easier if the island is once again under British rule. Let us watch for an opportunity. I would certainly welcome the influence on our own laws, if we are able to bring this back from Saint Lucia."

†

The harshness of the times did not spare anyone, and when yellow fever returned to the island in December of 1802, Kia feared she would lose Elizabeth to this incipient illness. The church bells tolled the number of victims, a constant reminder of the grisly loss of life. Few escaped almost immediate death. Kia's quiet sobs, as she lovingly stroked Elizabeth's forehead, reverberated against the stone walls.

"Kia, please bring Mr. Barlow. I'm afraid I haven't made proper provisions, for I have no will prepared." Elizabeth attempted to sit up, her insistence pushing through her fever-ravaged body.

"Shhh, my love." Kia continued her ministrations.

Except when making tea or bringing a new cloth to wipe Elizabeth's forehead, Kia never left her lover's side. When Elizabeth was overwhelmed with nausea and began to vomit, Kia brought the basin to her and held her hair. Kia continued her loving strokes until an exhausted Elizabeth lay back onto the mattress and fell into a fitful sleep.

Kia's fright increased when she saw the blood ooze from Elizabeth's mouth, nose, and eyes. She had tried to keep her worry from Elizabeth, but in one of Elizabeth's more lucid moments she saw the concern and once again called for the solicitor.

"Kia, please, I will not survive this, and I need to know you will be cared for," she pleaded.

Resolute in her belief that Elizabeth would not be taken away from her, Kia answered, "I will not let the fever win. You must drink the tea, Elizabeth, and stay strong. I love you so, and I would not wish to go on without you."

Elizabeth's tears mixed with blood as she began to cry. "Please, don't say that. I love you too. I always have. I will do my best to fight this, so we can continue to cherish our time together on earth."

There was nothing left to do, but pray. "Please, my Lord, do not take Elizabeth from me. I know that you cannot be that cruel. Your love for us shines through during the most difficult times. I trust you will give me the strength to endure and to help my love heal," Kia whispered, as her head bent over Elizabeth's frail body.

Kia didn't realize when Cissy, Rebecca, and Abraham had silently entered the room, until they all joined her in prayer. Elizabeth was a well-loved woman, even more than her father. Her selfless work with children and generous donations had saved many families from ruin. Without her generosity, there would have been far more deaths on the island, when the people suffered through drought, disease, and storms.

Three hands made contact with Kia. Cissy and Rebecca touched her shoulders on each side. Abraham, the steadying force, gently pressed his hand against her back for support and encouragement. The murmur of all four voices blended together in prayer.

Rebecca broke the quiet pleas with her soft voice. "Kia, let me bring you something to eat, while you insist on your quiet vigil. When Elizabeth throws the fever from her body, she will not want to worry about your own decline into poor health."

"Thank you, Rebecca," was all Kia was able to utter in response to Rebecca's kind gesture.

Kia suspected the trio finally left to allow herself and Elizabeth their solitude, even though all three had become family over the years. Saying farewell was a private affair. She kept her tears inside and remained strong for Elizabeth, refusing to believe her love would not survive.

After a day and night of praying and continued encouragement to drink the special tea, Elizabeth's eyes opened. Kia knew the fever had finally passed. Blue was replacing the red.

"Do not look so worried, my love. I believe I have made it through the worst of the fever. Perhaps some cool fresh water?"

Kia quickly stood to fetch the water and sent a silent prayer of thanks that her God answered her prayers. This was the final acknowledgment of His love and her belief in the righteousness of their affections. He had spared Elizabeth when so many others had not survived.

CHAPTER FOURTEEN

Elizabeth was reassessing her promise to Cissy to find passage for a visit with Captain Blythe; she saw Kia's reluctance to step into the sloop. Mr. Manu had offered to take them and Elizabeth thought it was a good way to show she had completely recovered from the fever and was well enough to make the journey. She'd learned the British had once again taken possession of the island, and from the news she was able to gather, there was an indication the island was stable. She was delighted to hear the rebels had escaped capture and established their own communities deep in the thick rain forests.

"Kia, my love, we do not have to make the journey. I can see your fear."

"So many years have passed. Why have I not forgotten by now? We cannot disappoint Cissy. Besides, I never properly thanked Captain Blythe for coming to my aide, not once, but twice. We cannot be rude and refuse her generous invitation. I will endure the journey as long as you are by my side." Kia looped her arm through Elizabeth's, and together they stepped onto the ship.

Cissy bounded on to the boat, eager to make the sailing and see the object of her infatuation. Elizabeth thought Cissy would be disappointed when she realized that Miss DuPont had captured the handsome captain's heart. There would, undoubtedly, be no other for Captain Blythe.

Elizabeth paid Mr. Manu a large sum to provide passage and afforded him the opportunity to make a more leisurely sail to his old friend's small piece of land. Mr. Manu made every effort to ensure they had a smooth sailing, but Elizabeth was relieved when land was spotted. Although the winds were gentle, Elizabeth did not take well to the swells in the sea and reliving a certain part of her bout with the fever. To see the new concern in Kia's eyes nearly broke her heart, and no amount of reassurance was sufficient to calm her fears.

Captain Blythe met the small group at the harbor, and her welcoming smile immediately put Elizabeth at ease.

"Captain Blythe, so good of you to meet us," Elizabeth greeted.

"Miss Allen, I am no longer a captain, you must call me Hillary. Since retirement, I've no use for the silly British formalities." Hillary reached her hand to steady Elizabeth on the uneven planks, when her footing caught the edge of a piece of wood.

"Hillary?" Elizabeth questioned. "That is an unusual name for an Englishwoman."

Hillary laughed. "Ah, yes, my father was quite enamored with Greece and perhaps with a certain Greek woman. I don't believe my mother was very pleased with his choice of name, but my father was a formidable man."

Elizabeth watched, as Kia's eyes traveled to the scar on the captain's cheek, but knew Kia would not be impolite to ask. She hoped Cissy would exercise as much restraint. Perhaps, Hillary would share the tale of how she obtained the small mark and once again entertain an enraptured Cissy. She remembered the small patch on Hillary's eye when she had come to their aid. At the time, she had been more concerned about Kia's well-being and failed to inquire about the injury.

"Wonderful, I believe I shall enjoy this rest very much. Please, call me Elizabeth."

"Cissy, you have grown into a beautiful woman. And who is this delightful creature?" Hillary turned her attention to Kia, who remained by Elizabeth's side as they greeted their host.

Cissy blushed. "Thank you, Captain Blythe."

"Hillary," she reminded.

"You remember Kia. The rescued African who was unjustly jailed as a runaway. She is my beloved companion." Elizabeth gestured to Kia.

"It is a great honor to be able to thank you for saving my life in so many more ways than merely pulling my body from the sea." Kia bowed her head slightly. "I remember when you brought some of us on deck to throw the chains into the sea."

Hillary nodded. "Kia, I'm afraid I don't recognize you, so great is your metamorphosis. I do, however, remember when the chains were tossed into the sea and the look on George Mitchell's face when I took my first step on the dock after you were released." Hillary chuckled. "Come, Mary has prepared a great meal for all of us, and Cecilia is so looking forward to your visit. I'm afraid she misses her family and some of the social gatherings from Savannah."

†

If Elizabeth had any doubts about the nature of Hillary's relationship with Cecelia DuPont, those doubts quickly disappeared. Cecilia's eyes lit up when the captain approached. Elizabeth noted the presence of several houses, and wondered if Hillary and Cecilia shared their small slice of heaven set among the mountainous region and circled with banana and coconut trees—two of Elizabeth's favorite fruits.

"Cecelia, I've forced our guests to discard all formalities. I hope you approve." Hillary smiled.

"Of course, I do. It's taken many years to tease away that stiffness you British are so well known for." Cecelia's southern drawl oozed from her mouth like warm honey, and Elizabeth instantly liked the beautiful woman. She accepted Cecelia's offered hand. "So good of you to come for a visit, you must be Elizabeth."

"Yes, and this is my companion, Kia, and our good friend, Cissy." Elizabeth made the introductions.

Cecelia's smile grew when Elizabeth introduced Kia as her companion. "Oh, I've heard many stories about Cissy, but none of Kia. We shall have to fix that. I hope you like fried chicken. Mary offered to cook up a large batch, which was a blessing. She's a far better cook than I. She was eager to meet you as well. We've planned a sort of party in your honor." Elizabeth was warmed by how Cecelia's southern hospitality extended to Kia and Cissy.

As the meal progressed, Elizabeth was impressed by the genuine interactions between what appeared to be Hillary's extended family and Cecelia. Anthony Page and his new bride folded seamlessly into the small group. There was no distinction between the two hosts, their guests, and the Africans, Mary and Joseph.

With a twinkle in her eye, Cecelia asked, "Tell us the story of how you and Kia became companions."

Elizabeth blushed. "Kia is one of the rescued Africans. When Hillary brought the group to me, I opened my house to her, as many of my congregation opened their houses to the others. Neither of us ever married, and it just made sense to continue our mission work side by side. Kia has a keen mind, and together, we teach the children of the island. I am afraid I would be lost without Kia."

"Not nearly as bereft as I would be without you, Elizabeth. Recently, Elizabeth gave us all a scare when she caught the fever," Kia added. "I don't think I would be able to teach the children without Elizabeth by my side."

Cecilia smiled, as she glanced at Hillary and exchanged a secret look. "Oh, so you both are teachers. We have much to talk about. I am a teacher as well. This is something that brings me a great many rewards and adds a kind of purpose I did not have in Savannah. Had I stayed there, I might have fallen into the sedentary life with no devotion other than arranging parties."

Hillary boldly leaned over and kissed Cecelia's cheek. Elizabeth was surprised by the openness of their affection for one another. As her gaze met Kia's, she noted this was not lost on her lover. Mary, Joseph, Anthony, and his wife did not seem to judge their interaction as unnatural. Elizabeth felt a freedom among these people that she had not quite experienced before, outside of Cissy and Rebecca's greater acceptance.

Both Cissy and Rebecca had bluntly brought the issue to the forefront, stating they simply believed there was no sin ever attached to love in whatever form that affection took between two women. She had allowed herself to relax around her two closest friends after that conversation.

After Cecelia's brazen question, Cissy must have felt released from propriety. With a grin, she blurted out, "Tell us the story of your scar, Hillary."

Hillary touched her cheek and smiled. "Ah, not such a grand tale but perhaps worth telling, because the ending was a fine one. The cowardly overseer, Morgan, had the audacity to accuse me of stealing his merchandise. To my misfortune, he had a belly full of rum and a pistol. The two are not an advised combination. The ball grazed my cheek, and Mary tended to me. I now bear the scar as a reminder. The mark is a pleasing remembrance of the lives saved."

"Oh my, were you frightened Cecelia? That must have worried you so."

Cecelia winked at Hillary. "I was more concerned when I saw the eye patch. I thought my dear captain had finally become a pirate, and I feared they would hunt her down and hang her from the nearest tree."

"Aye, the pirate's life for me." Hillary smiled. "Mary thought it best to wrap my entire head in a bandage since I had fallen and hit my head on the cobblestones. I thought for sure the ball had left me blind in one eye. I was thankful to escape the ordeal without the loss of sight, but that did not keep my crew from making merriment at my expense."

"I thought you looked quite dashing with your eye patch," Cecelia remarked.

The twinkle in Cecelia's eyes was a delight for Elizabeth to see, despite what she suspected was a very worrisome time for the two women. She hoped that Kia would eventually settle after their own brush with yellow fever.

"Tell us another story from when you were the captain," Cissy pleaded.

"Oh, I think that Page has more stories to tell. Mine are old and worn." She laughed.

"No, no, you will not use that excuse again. Let us tell the tales together," Page added. "I do believe it is time to tell the story about how we almost became true pirates. This seems like a group who might appreciate that tale."

"Will you, Mr. Page and Hillary? I do wish to hear that tale." Cissy's eyes brightened with excitement.

The rest of the evening was filled with tales of their time at sea and new stories of their life on Saint Lucia. Hillary proved to be a fine storyteller, weaving in her many adventures and keeping her guests amused.

When it was time to retire for the evening, Cecelia wore a sly smile when she informed them their home was not large enough to provide a separate bedroom for all three guests. "Elizabeth, would you and Kia mind sharing a room?" Elizabeth breathed a sigh of relief, knowing that Kia would worry if they were separated in the evenings.

†

Over the next several days, Elizabeth's health continued to improve, until she felt as if the yellow fever had never ravaged her body. On the last night, everyone stayed awake until well past dark enjoying their conversation and lamenting that the visitors would set sail and return to

Antigua the next day. Elizabeth offered to repay their kindness and hoped that one day she would be able to host any who wished to visit Antigua. She wasn't looking forward to the swell of the seas and the motion sickness it brought her. She would never choose to spend much time on the sea.

Kia nuzzled against Elizabeth's neck in the middle of the night and murmured, "I am so glad I faced my fear of the sea and made this journey with you. To see the color return to your cheeks and a sense of peace about you has brought me great joy. This trip has been exactly what the doctor ordered. I hope the sea sickness will not return as we journey home."

"Once we reach land, I will be fine. I wish Cecelia and Hillary lived closer to us. Being around the two of them has been an enlightening experience. I do feel terrible for Cissy. She's had such an infatuation with Hillary, and now that she sees her with Cecelia, her hopes are dashed."

"Perhaps, but now the way is paved for a certain young woman who hangs on every word, hoping for Cissy to notice her." Elizabeth could feel Kia's smile against her neck.

"Ah, so you've noticed as well. I do not think we should encourage anything. Let things unfold on their own."

"I wouldn't dream of it, my love."

"Oh, yes you would. You've far fewer internal struggles than I, and that's what I love most about you. Your devotion to the Lord and ability to accept love in all its glorious forms helped me see the light." Elizabeth turned to Kia and pressed their lips together.

"You would have gotten there on your own, eventually. I do so love you."

"And I you. I am no longer afraid to share my love with you."

CHAPTER FIFTEEN

Samuel Barlow had not survived the inveterate strain of yellow fever, and when Elizabeth returned to Antigua, she went directly to the solicitor's office to pay her respects to William. His eyes never lost their sadness after Samuel passed away. Although Samuel left William well cared for, it took another five years for him to establish himself as a solicitor, his grief too great to move on.

Though Elizabeth knew the risk, she was determined to wait until William was able to prepare her will. As she hurried to his office, she overheard the drone of voices and knew something momentous was occurring. Stepping inside, Elizabeth was delighted to see that William's grief had finally dissipated. When she noted the sparkle in his eyes, the source was immediately apparent. Not only had William completed his education, but he had hired a new clerk to assist in the blossoming need for services.

William stood and waved her inside. "Miss Allen, it is a delight to see you. Do you require our services again?"

"Yes Mr. Barlow and..." Elizabeth turned her gaze on the young man sitting on the right.

"Let me introduce my new clerk, Mr. Shaw."

Elizabeth nodded. "Mr. Shaw. Yes, I've put this off for far too long. I need you to prepare my will. I was fortunate to survive the fever..." She immediately regretted her words, knowing this reminder might cause William pain.

"It is fine, Miss Allen. Five years have passed. That is a long time. Please, sit." William motioned to the empty chair.

"Is something happening? I noted a distinct buzz of activity before entering this office."

"Ah yes, indeed. The House of Commons has passed an act to abolish the slave trade."

"Will the slaves be set free now?" Elizabeth asked in excitement.

"No, but this is the first major step. There are many more influential men who oppose slavery. It is only a matter of time," William answered. "Now, shall we prepare your will? I suspect you intend to leave most of your fortune to Miss Kia. Do you think it appropriate to give Miss Kia your last name? I can arrange for that as well."

Elizabeth frowned. "I've never considered that. I shall ask Kia if that is her wish."

William smiled. "I believe she would be honored to take your last name, as I was to take Samuel's. I know of the many jokes made at our expense, but that did not change my wish to take his last name."

"Thank you, Mr. Barlow. And yes, I do wish to ensure that the majority of my wealth be passed along to Kia, with some additional provisions made for Cissy, Abraham and his family, and the church, of course."

"Of course."

✝

As Kia and Elizabeth were strolling arm in arm along the path around their home, Cissy walked slowly toward them. Rheumatism had not been kind to her joints, and Cissy was now past her prime. She'd acquired a certain amount of acclaim with her children's books and had attracted her own companion nearly twenty years prior. Elizabeth was pleased she would not move into an advanced age without someone to love. The woman who lived with Cissy was several years younger but no less devoted than Kia was to Elizabeth.

Elizabeth smiled at Kia who was still a beautiful woman, despite the gray that had made its way into the tight curls on her head. Although she kept her hair cropped close to the scalp, the silver shined through. The tiny wrinkles around her eyes were far less prominent than the ones on Elizabeth's own face, but Kia also insisted Elizabeth's beauty would carry on well past her prime.

"The day has finally come." Cissy looked to the sky and brought her hands together.

"What are you mumbling about, Cissy?" Elizabeth asked.

"I had hoped this day would come sooner, after the Slave Trade Act in 1807, but men procrastinate far more than women and it has taken an additional twenty-seven years for this wrong to right."

"Do you mean to tell us that slavery has been abolished?" Kia asked.

"Yes, and it only took an additional year after the House of Commons passed the act." Cissy replied wryly. "All the plantation owners have given their slaves immediate freedom, laying aside all claims to apprenticeship."

"I am happy to have survived so long to see this transpire. I have only one more request before I die. I yearn to lay buried next to Kia. I do wish there was a way to achieve that final invocation."

"Mr. Gilbert, Abraham, has an idea." Kia's eyes twinkled.

"So, you have been conspiring with Mr. Gilbert?" Elizabeth's brow rose.

"A family cemetery. The land is his and there is a lovely place overlooking the hills. When the moon shines down, there is nothing more beautiful," Kia answered.

"He would allow us to lie side by side in his family plot?"

"Abraham assures me he would be honored. He has long considered us both family but was not presumptuous enough to believe you shared his view or that you would wish to lie somewhere other than where your father rests."

"All of you are my family. You, Cissy, the Gilberts, that was never a question. I am pained my father will not lie with us. I believe he would have wished for that, but I will not desecrate his grave and move him." Elizabeth placed her hand on Kia's cheek. "I have long since resolved my internal reflection, my place is beside you."

Kia placed her hand on top of Elizabeth's leaning into the touch. "And I with you."

Cissy moved away and did not intrude on their private moment.

"I shall pray that I go before you, because I cannot live without you by my side. I will surely die soon after of a broken heart," Elizabeth declared.

"Our years together have been many. Of that I am most thankful," Kia responded. "The slave trade is a terrible injustice, and I am glad it has been abolished. Yet, I will never be sorry I was taken from my village, for that brought me to you. I am loathe to say this, because so many others were not as fortunate as I was."

"I understand and feel the same way. To think that love blossomed from such a tragedy. The human spirit is strong when paired with the purity of love."

"We are foolish old women, aren't we?" Kia asked.

"Yes, but foolish old women in love for nearly forty years, who were brave enough to embrace our love."

"Perhaps not so foolish then." Kia leaned over and kissed Elizabeth, who patted Kia's wrinkled cheek.

EPILOGUE

June 2017

The two women laughed in the salt breeze, as their hair whipped around their heads. They'd just taken a hike in the hills, and their arms were swinging as their hands were clasped together. One a chocolate brown and another a bright red, peppered with tiny freckles.

Roxanne had used every ounce of persuasion, including special attention to Lorraine's sweet center. During a particularly weak moment, Lorraine had agreed to spend their honeymoon on Antigua. While they basked in the aftermath of lovemaking, Roxanne had pleaded and Lorraine acquiesced.

"Now, aren't you happy we came here?"

"Hmmm, maybe, but if you don't slather more sunscreen on those lobster arms of yours, I won't be able to have my wicked ways with you," Lorraine teased.

"Aloe works wonders."

"I still don't understand why you wanted to come to this backward location. I read that Antigua was one of the worst places to live if you're gay. For shit's sake, they passed a law in 1995 regulating the sexual acts of two consenting adults with a prison sentence up to fifteen years. Jesus, they even kept the old 1533 term for the act, calling it buggery. And if that isn't enough to convince you, even after Parliament insisted the ban on sodomy was antiquated and should be appealed, the government announced it had no intention of repealing the ban."

"We have sodomy laws in the States, but I still want to visit those places," Roxanne argued.

"Maybe we shouldn't. I say we boycott every backwater place in America that continues to discriminate against our community. It seems like that's the only thing that ever works. Hit them in their pocketbooks."

Roxanne abruptly kissed Lorraine and smiled up at her. "That's why I fell madly in love with you. Your passion and activism is so damned hot."

"And you don't fight fair. Come on, if we're going to play tourist, we'd better get a move on. I love visiting the old grave sites. That was another thing. Did you know they didn't allow blacks and whites to mingle in their cemeteries?"

"I'm quite sure that happened in the States too. We shouldn't be so self-righteous about where we live. At least they abolished slavery here more than thirty years before us, and it didn't take a frickin' war to accomplish that. You're not the only one who researches history. Besides, I have a special treat for you with this tour we're going on. I really had to dig, too. I wanted to find the perfect excursion for us. You have to admit, it's really beautiful here."

"Okay, lead the way you little, master manipulator," Lorraine grumbled with a tiny smile.

†

The young woman met them at the hotel, and Lorraine was surprised to learn that Roxanne had arranged a private tour of a family cemetery. The woman was striking, her beauty highlighted even more through her colorful island attire. Lorraine was not about to change her behavior, screw it if the inhabitants of the island disapproved of her marriage to Roxanne. She would hold her wife's hand in defiance, odd looks be damned. But the woman did not blink an eye at their clasped hands. In contrast, she smiled broadly when meeting them in the lobby.

"Congratulations to the two of you. I am so happy to meet you both. My family has lived on this island for many generations, and the story I am about to tell was passed down from mother to son or daughter to ensure honor is paid to our adopted family."

"Adopted family?" Lorraine asked.

"Come, you will see. I have my car waiting."

Lorraine and Roxanne climbed into the shining, black Toyota Avensis. Lorraine had noticed a definite preference for Japanese made vehicles on the island.

After a short drive along the bumpy road, the three women arrived at their destination. Lorraine was eager to see the old cemetery. Her fascination with historical gravesides was something she shared with Roxanne. Both women appreciated the rich history they could glean from looking at the writing on the stone markers. Their friends always thought they were a match made in heaven, with their gruesome shared interest in old cemeteries. Lorraine had once confessed that she fell in love with Roxanne the moment she suggested they visit the Roslyn cemetery on their first date.

This family cemetery was a lot older than Lorraine had imagined, and dated as far back as 1840. The engraving on the stones marking the deaths of two women separated by one day caught her attention. She looked at the beautiful tour guide in wonder.

> Elizabeth Allen
> August 7, 1768 - April 8, 1850
> Devoted missionary, friend and companion to Kia
Allen
> Kia Allen
> Unknown - April 9, 1850
> Devoted missionary, friend and companion to Elizabeth Allen
> "Where you go I will go, and where you stay I will stay. Your people will be my people and your God my God. Where you die I will die, and there I will be buried."

The guide smiled and began speaking, "It is a beautiful story I am about to tell. Elizabeth Allen was British and a Methodist missionary who devoted her entire life and fortune to the education of the island inhabitants, mostly former slaves and free Africans. Soon after her father died, who was also a missionary, she bequeathed her land to my ancestor, Abraham Gilbert, for the sum of one pound. A ridiculous amount in those times. The ten acres were worth much more, and my ancestor was himself a freed slave."

"But who was Kia Allen?" Lorraine asked.

"Ah, that is the beautiful part of the story. Kia was African royalty. She had been captured by slave traders and left to die on an abandoned ship in the midst of a raging storm. A female captain rescued a group of about twenty women and children, and brought them to Elizabeth and her father, John."

"A woman? No way. I know there were female pirates, but a female captain?" Lorraine asked.

"Oh yes, Captain Hillary Blythe was well known in these parts, but that is an entirely different story that you must remind me to tell you about. Let's return to the women who lie side by side in this gravesite. Kia remained with Elizabeth from 1795 to her death in 1850."

Roxanne smiled. "They were lovers?"

"They were. Elizabeth made provision in her will that Kia, with the exception of a small sum earmarked for my ancestors, inherited her entire fortune, which at the time was a very large sum. Although Kia was an old woman, her health was still good. She is rumored to have died of a broken heart after her beloved Elizabeth passed away. With no one else to receive her fortune, Abraham's great granddaughter, Kia Gilbert, became a very rich young girl."

"Another Kia?" Roxanne asked.

"Yes, a namesake. This practice was common with my ancestors. They often honored their adopted family by naming their children after members of the Allen family. I believe there is also an Anne somewhere in my family tree, named after Elizabeth's mother. And of course, there are several Elizabeths. We like to recycle names. I myself am a namesake; I am named after Abraham's wife, Rebecca."

"Wow! Yeah, I see all the gravestones here." Lorraine exclaimed, as she walked around.

"Since Elizabeth and Kia died within one day of the other, the stipulation in both of their wills that they be laid to rest side by side was easy to accommodate. This was unheard of at the time, but there was nothing that could be done, since they were laid to rest on my family's land. It is rumored that young Kia hovered around the two women, clinging to their skirts and listening to every word they uttered. She became a very prominent woman in the community, and quite formidable if there was any scandalous talk of the two women after their passing."

"That's an amazing story. Too bad this island does not embrace love in the same way as your ancestors seem to have easily accepted," Lorraine stated.

The guide nodded sadly. "Yes, you are correct, but we will not give up the fight. Someday, our laws will mirror your country."

"I'm not so sure you should aspire to the standards of the States. Little by little, we are at risk of losing everything and taking a giant step backward. I do hope that doesn't happen, but I have to be realistic and continue to fight." Lorraine met the guide's eyes.

"I come here when I am most discouraged and read the words on the stone. That always lifts my spirits. I hope it has done the same for you."

Lorraine placed a gentle kiss on Roxanne's lips. "Okay, honey, you win. This was the perfect place to honeymoon. I'll never forget that beautiful story. Thank you."

"I plan to spend the next sixty years or so seeking out all those historical tales that show how love always wins out, despite the many challenges," Roxanne answered. "Rest in peace and love, Elizabeth and Kia."

ABOUT THE AUTHOR

Ali Spooner

Ali Spooner, a native of Florida, now calls Pensacola her forever home. Ali has been writing for many years as a hobby, and with the assistance of the Affinity Rainbow Publishing team, has taken her love of storytelling to a new level.

Ali's characters range from cowgirls and psychics, to a healthy dose of supernatural beings. She has written stand-alone titles and series. Ali is an avid reader and her other hobbies include photography, outdoor activities and watching college sports.

Annette Mori

Annette is an award winning author and health care executive living in the beautiful Pacific Northwest with her wife and their five furry kids. She has ten published novels including Goldie award winner, *Locked Inside*. The positive feedback has spurred her on and she is thankful to have the support of so many wonderful readers. Feel free to drop her a line at: annettemori0859@gmail.com, sign up for her mailing list at: http://eepurl.com/cS3amj, or check out her blog at: https://annettemori0859.wordpress.com/

OTHER AFFINITY BOOKS

Kai's Heart by Renee MacKenzie
The time has come for the Resistance to take back control of
New America from the Anointed tyrants. Growing up the
daughter of a Resistance Army General, Kai Brodie's focus
is keenly on the upcoming Revolution. So how is it then that
she can't take her eyes off the beautiful Anointed guard?
Rachel Hart's amber-gold eyes reflecting back at her all of
the unanswered questions about the true goals of the
Resistance. Will Kai and Rachel survive the battle over the
fate of their beloved New America?

Diamond Dreams by Ali Spooner
Cameron St. Angelo dreams of playing softball in the
College World Series. Earning a scholarship to play ball for

her beloved LSU brings Cam one-step closer to achieving this dream. When Cam arrives on campus, she joins a family of women who share her love of the sport, and she realizes there is room in her life for another love.

Unconventional Lovers by Annette Mori
Bri and Siera are young women with huge hearts and strong wills; they want nothing more than to find a peaceful and secure space to be themselves. But the world is a harsh place for anyone who is different. Bri's Aunt Olivia is a vet who channels her emotions into her work and her love of Bri. Siera has her Aunt Deb who adores her. Despite their individual battles against hurt, prejudice and rejection, can these four women find love against the odds?

Say You Won't Go by JM Dragon & Erin O'Reilly
Logan Perry spent part of an inheritance traveling to various states, unconsciously looking for something to focus her life on. Taryn Donovan has no self-esteem and hates the waitressing job that barely keeps her in food. Can an unexpected weekend encounter turn out to be something more fulfilling? Find out in this sexually charged romance.

Playing with Matches by Lacey Schmidt
Dr Augusta Stuart has devoted her adult life to supporting the mental health of disadvantaged children and moves to a new clinic in San Antonio. Her friend sets her up on a date with Callia Alexana. Prickly debates are somehow as unexpectedly fascinating as playing with matches, and Gus is forced to consider what preconceptions she is willing to burn to find true love.

Changing Perspectives by Jen Silver
Art director, Dani Barker, lives life on the edge and finance director Camila Callaghan thinks it's necessary to stay in the closet to maintain her position. When Dani and Camila meet, they both sense an attraction, A change of perspective for both women is needed if they are to act on it.

Death is Only the Beginning by JM Dragon
What would you do if you were in a fatal accident with a stranger and ended up in heaven with them? Only to find out it wasn't an accident, it was murder. Follow the ghostly adventures of these two acrimonious strangers, who help two women find love and find closure for their predicament.

For the Love of a Woman by S. Anne Gardner
Enter a world where oil is supreme, passion rules reason and there is always the threat of civil war. In this jungle of power Raisa Andieta resides as one of its masters. Her only desire is to rule it alone. Carolyn Stenbeck is just trying to keep her marriage together. Her only desire is to be able to escape and never look back. When Raisa and Carolyn meet, it is like fuel and fire…a storm is brewing. Civil War is in the air, and passion like the coming storm begins to erupt.

The Bee Charmer by Ali Spooner
After the death of her father, Nat St. Croix needs to decide on which direction her life should take. Does she continue her life alone, as a trapper and trader, or does she start over and try to fit into a town surrounded by strangers? Will the call of the wild and all that is familiar win out, or will the call of love capture Nat's heart?

Affinity
Rainbow Publications

eBooks, Print, Free eBooks

Visit our website for more publications available online.

www.affinityrainbowpublications.com

Published by Affinity Rainbow Publications
A Division of Affinity eBook Press NZ LTD
Canterbury, New Zealand

Registered Company 2517228

CPSIA information can be obtained
at www.ICGtesting.com
Printed in the USA
LVHW081748141220
674152LV00036B/832